Caro froze for a fa.... ...
shock, before twisting round to level ...
Horra grazed past her in a characteristic attack and its
major tentacles, trailing behind the conical body, snaked
around Caro, pinning her arms to her sides. She was
upside down in relation to the Horra, and Myrah caught
a glimpse of the ghastly organic spear of its sexual arm
stabbing upwards into Caro's throat. Caro's body
convulsed and suddenly the water all around was
stained with arterial blood. The Horra, with its
propulsion siphon jetting spasmodically, circled back
towards its hiding place. Its course took it near the
centre of the group and one of the men, Toms, lunged at
it with his spear. The Horra shrilled in pain . . .

**Also by Bob Shaw in VGSF.**

**NIGHT WALK**

# BOB SHAW

# Medusa's Children

**VGSF**

VGSF is an imprint of Victor Gollancz Ltd
14 Henrietta Street, London WC2E 8QJ

First published in Great Britain 1977
by Victor Gollancz Ltd

First VGSF edition 1987

Copyright © Bob Shaw 1977

*British Library Cataloguing in Publication Data*
Shaw, Bob
    Medusa's children.
    I. Title
    823'.914[F]        PR6069.H364

ISBN 0-575-04096-3

Printed and bound in Great Britain
by Richard Clay (The Chaucer Press) Ltd, Bungay, Suffolk

# Medusa's Children

# CHAPTER ONE

Myrah woke with a start, convinced she had heard a cry from one of the six babies in her care, but the nursery was quiet except for the steady breathing of the air pumps.

She remained quite still for a moment, while full consciousness returned, then decided to inspect each of the babies individually in case one of them had become ill or was caught in a freakish accretion of dead air. Unloosing the restraint cord from the fastening clip on her belt, she pushed herself away from the curved metal wall and floated low over the sleeping babies. They were in perfect repose, drifting comfortably at the ends of their short tethers, absurd little faces registering contentment or lordly boredom. The air currents induced by Myrah's passage across the nursery caused the babies to rock and wallow slightly, like flowers nodding in a breeze, but they remained asleep. She checked her flight by grasping the bracket of a storage net and launched herself back to her original position close to the room's circular window.

It took only a few seconds for Myrah to secure the restraint cord to the braided belt which was her sole item of apparel. She was wide awake now, the notion that her charges might have been in danger having driven out all desire for sleep, but there was no point in leaving the nursery until another watcher arrived for a duty spell. Close to Myrah's face, on the moisture-beaded wall, was a sawn-off bracket which had once held a run of copper pipes. The pipes had long since been removed, probably for the fashioning of spears, but underneath the fixture there remained a rectangular brass plate. It was engraved with the words: TORPEDO HOIST—H.P. HYDRAULICS.

Myrah traced the letters with a finger-tip, as she had done many times before, wondering about the meaning they must have had for the Clan's founders. Tiring of the speculation, she closed her eyes and tried to go to sleep again, but at that moment there came a faint cry from one of the sentries outside. It contained a note of surprise or excitement, and she realised belatedly that it had been a similar sound which had wakened her.

She changed her position and pulled the circular window open, relying on the air pressure within the nursery to prevent water from billowing in. The world outside looked much as it always did—a pale blue universe of transparent water in which spherical air bubbles of all different sizes drifted like globes of silver foil. So plentiful were the bubbles this morning that they made it difficult to see much beyond the Home's protective nets, but this was not a particularly rare occurrence and offered no explanation for the sentry's call. Myrah held her breath and pushed her head into the gently undulating vertical surface of the water, hoping for a better view of what was going on. There was little to be seen on this side of the Home, except for nets and a column of root structure, and she withdrew her head from the water. As she was doing so, a strong hand gripped the inner surface of her thigh and pulled her further into the room.

"I could have had you like that," a male voice said. "Very tempting indeed."

Myrah twisted and saw Harld, a fair-haired youth from the Hunting family, who had entered the nursery with a professional lack of noise. He was a pleasant-natured boy, with a lithe body which bore very few of the Horra scars which so often made hunters look ugly. Myrah had swum with him many times.

She smiled at him. "So early in the morning! You must be eating well."

"I am." He caught hold of her restraint cord and, using

6

it as an anchor line, drew his body closer to hers. "But I'm still hungry—I think I could eat you all up."

Myrah allowed their bodies to touch for a moment, as a normal gesture of courtesy, then pushed him away. "Not here in the nursery," she said. "I'll swim with you later today if you want."

He shook his head. "I'm not going for ice."

"Why not? I thought you had been chosen."

"We got no kingfish yesterday. Solman says we've to hunt again today, and I've also to take the early spell in here for five days—as a punishment."

Myrah instantly detached herself from the wall and made ready to leave. "The nursery watch isn't a punishment."

Harld nodded without conviction and looked at the six babies, some of whom were beginning to stir at the sound of voices. The sponge bags tied between their legs, to prevent their excretions of the night drifting through the room, showed signs of staining. "I see you haven't cleaned them."

"First watch always does that."

"And you say this isn't a punishment duty!" Harld rolled his eyes in a good-humoured display of exasperation and unfastened the straps of his bubble cage from around his forehead. "I suppose I'd better get started."

"Yes, and remember to be gentle with them." Myrah took her own bubble cage from the nearest storage net and strapped it on. Its filigrees of chiselled bone curved around her head like the petals of a huge flower.

"I'll take care," Harld said. "For all I know, one of them could be mine." While he was speaking one of the babies gave a thin, irritated squawk.

"Probably that one," Myrah bantered.

"He isn't handsome enough." Harld wedged his feet into loops on the floor, to give himself working leverage, and untied the baby which had cried out. "Have any of them been coughing?"

"Of course not—I'd have heard." Myrah tried to suppress a pang of unease. "You shouldn't talk about coughing in here."

7

Harld looked at her in amused surprise. "Talking about it doesn't bring it on."

"I know, but...." She decided to change the subject. "What's happening outside? I heard somebody shouting."

"I didn't notice. I came here on the inner path."

"Why weren't you able to get any kingfish yesterday?"

"Solman says it's because we didn't try hard enough, but I think it's something to do with the new current. Their feeding ground could have changed."

Myrah nodded thoughtfully and kicked off towards the doorway of the nursery. Her accurately judged trajectory took her into the corridor beyond. There was less light here, but she was familiar with this part of the Home and two more impulsions brought her quickly to an outer doorway through which streamed the azure light of the morning. The surface of the water, held in check by air pressure, curved and flattened like a glassy blanket. She went into it head first and swam away to the right. On her third stroke she picked up a large bubble by putting her face into it and allowing its surface tension to glue it into the spherical framework of her cage. The action was performed automatically, almost as a reflex. Myrah could swim a long way before needing to breathe—and she was going to a section of the Home which was near at hand—but she had been conditioned since childhood to capture any air which became available.

Taking the free breath, she swam towards the central region of the Home, in the direction she thought of as up. She knew that when any solid object was released in an air space it eventually drifted down, but this movement was so gradual, and so easily reversed by air currents, that it played virtually no part in her spatial orientation. Up was the general direction from which light came during the day, and it was most easily identified by reference to the branching root structures which reached all the way to the surface of the world. Multiple columns of these roots stretched above her now, providing a shadowy background to the clustered buildings of the Home which hung motionless in the water like

8

dead whales. At this level, near the bottom of the euphotic zone, reds and greens were very weak, and Myrah was swimming in a luminous blue universe shot through with galaxies of silver globes and darting fish.

She passed through an opening in the fine-mesh net which held the Home's communal air supply, and penetrated the air-water interface at a speed which sent her arcing across the giant bubble amid a spray of droplets. In spite of the earliness of the hour, she could see a knot of people gathered about the figure of a man who was wearing the metal bubble cage of a sentry. She hooked one hand around a guide rope, using the momentary contact to effect a change of direction, and came to rest near the edge of the group.

At close range she recognised the sentry as Shire, an older man from a neighbouring dormitory. He was holding a sea hare, which was obviously still alive. It was a type of giant slug which was regarded as a delicacy by the people of the Clan and which fed on algae near the surface. Members of ice-gathering parties usually tried to bring some back with them, but Myrah had never seen one roaming free in the deeps.

"Where did you get it?" she said. At the sound of her voice the group rearranged itself to give her access to the centre.

"It just drifted into my hands," Shire replied, obviously enjoying the attention. "I was on first watch at the Topeast entrance, and it just drifted into my hands."

"You're lucky. It should make good eating."

"Oh, I'm not going to eat it—not yet anyway." Shire grinned at the encircling faces. "I have to show it around first."

Myrah nodded and withdrew from the group in case Shire became aware of the pity she felt for him. He was an old man, fortyish, who would probably begin coughing any day now—provided his slowing reactions did not make him fall prey to the Horra, or even some less dangerous predator. All that lay before him was the prospect of dying and being forgotten, all that lay behind him was an unremarkable span

9

of unremarkable years—and yet for the moment he was as happy as a small child. The finding of the sea hare was a genuine high spot in his life, and the realisation of this filled Myrah with a profound sadness. It was difficult to see any point at all in the whole process of being born, living out one's life in the Home, and then dying and being allowed to drift slowly into the darkness at the centre of the world, where Ka was waiting....

"What's wrong, Myrah?" The words came from Lennar, another member of the Hunting family, who had taken up a position beside her. He was a little older than Harld and therefore, inevitably, had more scars on his arms and torso, but Myrah liked him for his steadiness and air of thoughtful maturity. It was expected that he would be offered the next vacancy on the Clan Council.

"It's old Shire," she said, taking Lennar's outstretched hand. "He makes me sick."

"Why?"

"He's swollen up like a puffer fish—and for what?"

"You should be pleased you're not like him."

"But how do I know I'm not? What's going to be my big achievement, Lennar?"

"Being alive is an achievement in itself," Lennar said. "It's enough for me—and I haven't even the prospect of giving birth."

Myrah caught his free hand, and they drifted in the air, facing each other. "All right, say I have a baby ... say I'm very lucky and have two and they both live ... where does that get me? Where does it get them?"

"I don't know, Myrah." Lennar gave her a rueful smile. "I only work on problems I think have a solution. Will you swim with me today?"

"If you want." Myrah let her gaze travel over his body, noting the contrast between the blackness of his hair and the whiteness of his skin, and knew she would like to have a son in the same mould. "When are we going?"

"Soon. Solman wants us to leave earlier than usual because of the new current."

This was the second time in the space of a few minutes that somebody had spoken to Myrah about a current and it began to dawn on her that it could have some significance. "What's so special about this current?"

"It's been moving steadily for three days, which is very unusual." Lennar freed one of his hands and pointed downwards. "And it's going that way. The world seems to be changing."

"You mean the current is flowing into the centre of the world?" Myrah thought briefly about Ka having developed the power to draw bodies towards himself at an even faster rate, but her mind shied away from the vision. "That doesn't make sense."

"We don't know where it's going—but it's persistent, and it doesn't seem to be circular like any other current. I think Solman is worried."

Myrah almost laughed. "He's getting too old."

Lennar showed no sign of being amused. "There's something not right about it, Myrah—look at the way that sea hare drifted right into Shire's hands. You never saw that happen before."

"Perhaps I wouldn't have noticed. It seems a very trivial event."

"All right," Lennar said. "Just take note when we go outside—you'll see the bubbles sinking down as well."

"The world is full of currents," Myrah snapped, appalled by the ideas Lennar seemed to be trying to put into her mind. "Are we going for ice, or aren't we?"

"Of course—we still have to drink."

"Let's go, then." Myrah turned away from Lennar, caught a guide rope and propelled herself upwards in the direction of the Topeast entrance, the point from which the ice-gathering parties always departed. She was one of the strongest members of the Artisan family, and could travel fast, but Lennar caught up with her at once.

"I'm sorry if I annoyed you," he said. "Are we still swimming together?"

"As long as you promise to talk sensibly."

"Promise." Lennar slid his hand through Myrah's belt and they made their way up through the vast netted bubble, moving their limbs in a steady rhythm. They passed dark holes which were entrances to some of the individual dwellings which made up the Home. The huge fish-like shapes of the houses could be seen beyond the net, partially obscured by shadows, reflections and offshoots of the root structure to which they were attached. Around the edge of each entrance the material of the net was carefully stitched or glued to the doorway so that none of the air passing into the house would slip away into the surrounding water.

A small child—pale, lonely figure—waved from one of the entrances as they passed by, and Myrah waved back, thinking of her own infancy when she too had sat and watched the hunters and the ice-gatherers as they worked their way up to an assembly point. The adults had seemed wise and strong to her in those days, god-like beings, masters of the luminous blue universe, and Myrah had looked forward to growing up and joining their ranks. That particular dream had come true—here she was, in full-breasted womanhood, setting off on one of the selfsame expeditions—but the purpose, the mysterious and glamorous purpose, seemed to have vanished with so many of her childhood preconceptions. Had they really, those pale-bodied warrior-kings and their consorts, been concerned with nothing more significant than the scavenging of pieces of ice to convert into drinkable water?

If so, if there was no more to it, what was the essential difference between a member of the Clan and any other of the myriad life forms which spawned and fought and died in the waters around the Home?

They reached the upper part of the bubble and went through the folds of fine mesh into the water. Four clean strokes took them upwards to a smaller trapped bubble which surrounded an opening in the outer defensive screen. Two young women, Caro and Geean, were waiting inside the bubble. They greeted Myrah and Lennar and issued them with short, tubular spears and bags made of cowfish skin. Other human figures could be seen treading water outside.

"How many are here?" Lennar folded his bag and tucked it through his belt.

"All ten of us, now that you're here," Caro said. "We're ready to go."

Lennar looked mildly surprised. "Such enthusiasm! I wish every team I led would pay as much attention to my instructions."

"Nobody's paying any attention to you," Caro said with a challenging smile. "It was Solman who put the fear of Ka into them. He's in a bad mood."

"I can get into bad moods too, you know." Lennar made an attempt to look ferocious.

"That must be very frightening." Caro's smile grew broader. "Will you swim with me?"

"I'm going up with Myrah, but I'll come back with you if you want."

Caro looked disappointed as she turned to Myrah. "I might have known you'd get in first. I don't know why you haven't been pregnant three times over."

Myrah considered explaining that Lennar had made the proposal, but decided it would seem too defensive. She was twenty-three years old and for some time now had been concerned over her apparent inability to contribute to the strength of her family. Caro, on the other hand, was a ripe-bodied seventeen-year-old, filled with confidence in her own fertility. She had set her sights on the rare prize of double motherhood and seemed likely to achieve her goal.

"There are other men going with us," Myrah said.

"I know, but I like Lennar." Caro gave him a direct smile.

"Swim with him, then—I'm not all that interested."

"Myrah, I asked you," Lennar said, showing some displeasure.

"I know you did." Myrah was unhappy about the way the

discussion was going, but she had decided to appear diffident—rather than compete with Caro—and was prepared to accept the consequences. "But today I'm not all that interested."

"All right, Myrah." Lennar gave her a look of concern before turning to Caro. "What about this early start we're supposed to be making? We're wasting too much time."

He checked the straps of his bubble cage, then led the way outside. Caro went closely behind him, with one hand tucked possessively into his belt, and Myrah and Geean followed. Geean gave Myrah a sympathetic glance, but she did not acknowledge it because that too would have been an admission that she had wanted to swim with Lennar. Privately, she hoped that this new mood of disillusionment and discontent would evaporate before it made her life any more complicated.

As soon as they were clear of the Home's defensive mesh the members of the group ranged themselves in a line for the obligatory inspection by the leader. Their bodies, naked except for the patterned belts denoting their families, reflected the blue morning light as they gently trod water, but in the virtual absence of gravity these movements were so slight that they could have been taken for an optical effect. The only noticeable breaks in the line occurred when a man or woman moved to ensnare a fresh air bubble from the hordes of silvery spheres which drifted all around. Myrah, positioned at one end of the line, noticed that the bubbles were indeed moving downwards, and her sense of unease returned in strength.

Lennar swam slowly along the line. He collected from each female a small tally which was her House Mother's testimony that she was near the midpoint of her menstrual cycle and therefore was unlikely to perfume the water with blood. The precaution was a vital one on all long-range forays, because some of the most dangerous predators could detect blood at great distances and were strongly attracted to it. Lennar then extracted from each member of the party a formal statement that he or she had not begun to cough—lung damage could

14

also result in blood passing into the water—and completed his inspection by assuring himself that nobody present had skin lacerations.

Satisfied that all was well, he gave a signal and the group began to swim upwards. The sentry at the Topeast entrance waved farewell to them and retired into the comfort of his bubble net.

As the indistinct outline of the Home sank away beneath them, the members of the group arranged themselves in traditional formation. Lennar and the other two men moved to a central position, and the three women with whom they had elected to swim closed in with them. As a necessary preliminary to sexual union, each pair linked themselves together by intertwining their belts, and then settled into the slow-surging, erotic rhythms of the swim. Their bubble cages were pressed together, symbolically uniting their air supplies. The four remaining women took up their stations in an outer circle, with the double duty of watching for possible dangers and occasionally steering large air bubbles towards the couples in the centre.

Myrah swam easily and economically, her spear held lightly between the thumb and forefinger of her right hand. As they moved up through the euphotic zone, hour after hour, the light grew stronger, and shades of red and green began to appear in the towering root column beside which they were travelling. At these levels there was very little chance of encountering any Horra, who preferred to roam the darkness, and Myrah found herself watching the three couples in the heart of the formation. The sight of men and women locked together at mouth, waist and loins was a familiar one to her. Fertility was low among the people of the Clan, mortality from many causes was high, and the only way they could maintain their numbers was by maximising the chances of conception.

In the past, observing the sexual play of men and women swimming together had always stimulated Myrah's own desire, but on this occasion, quite abruptly, she discovered in herself a profound emptiness. She watched Lennar and Caro with detachment. She noted the subtle way in which Caro some-times made her swimming strokes fractionally later than Lennar's so that the disparity in their movements reinforced his penetration of her body—and none of it meant anything to her. Even her sense of rivalry with Caro, a petty but human emotion, had faded away, leaving her as spent and lifeless as one of the fragile mollusc shells she sometimes saw drifting down into the dark heart of the world. The feeling was a new one for Myrah, and part of her mind was afraid of it, but there was nobody to whom she could turn for reassurance.

Moving her arms and legs automatically, trapped in her own intangible bubble of loneliness, she continued her slow progression to the surface.

# CHAPTER TWO

Hal Tarrant was eating a light supper consisting mainly of dried fruit and cereals, while seated at his usual place by the window.

The large, north-facing window was the best feature of his house, with its jewel-bright views of the island's green slopes and the ocean beyond. He kept a large table at it and liked to sit there for all meals and while attending to paperwork connected with the farm. Even when he was relaxing in the evenings he tended to sit at the table, rather than in an armchair, and cover it with his paraphernalia for relaxation—the books, the pipes and tobacco, the wine bottle and his single antique crystal glass.

As he chewed the unprocessed food, Tarrant's gaze moved continuously over the geometrical patterns of the algae beds which began close to the shore and extended almost to the horizon. An occasional boat still moved in the waterways which separated the beds, but the day's work was practically over and in the lingering red-gold light of the sunset the farm looked as peaceful as a private park.

It was a scene from which Tarrant normally derived comfort—the visible testimony that men could still work together—but on this evening his grey eyes were sombre and intent. Several times during the simple meal he picked up his binoculars and used them to identify farm boats as they drew in to the ragged line of jetties far below him. He was a tall man of thirty, with a spare, flat-chested build which would have made him look like a teenager had it not been for the adult identity, ratified by experience, which was impressed on his features. Each time he set the binoculars down his expression grew more thoughtful and the tension he was feeling became more apparent in the quick restless movements of his hands.

Finally, he pushed his plate away, went to a cupboard in the corner of the square room and took out a military-style rifle. The weapon was almost a hundred years old, but had been maintained in excellent condition. It was a good 23rd century copy of a late 20th century Armalite, and Tarrant had chosen it because it represented the highest point of one branch of technology. He had a fondness for good machines, whatever their purpose. From an upper shelf in the cupboard he took a box of cartridges he knew to be of practically the same quality as the rifle's original ammunition, and filled the magazine. He pulled on a lightweight jacket, slung the rifle over his shoulder and went out into the warm, heavy air of the evening.

It was growing dark, and yellow glimmers of electric light marked the positions of dwellings among the shrubs and trees. Tarrant walked quickly down the deserted hill, his long strides covering the ground silently and without effort. When he reached the jetties on the island's northern shore he was surprised to see there was still some activity on Will Somerville's blue-painted boat, *The Rose of York*, which was moored three berths along from his own. He paused for a moment, wondering why Somerville was working so late.

"Will?" he shouted. "Is that you? What are you doing down there?"

There was a sound of movement and a clinking of glass below deck, then Somerville's bearded face appeared in the hatchway. "I'm trying to save you some time and money," he said gruffly, feigning annoyance at the interruption. He was a thick-set man of fifty who affected a piratical red bandana in place of a hat to protect his balding head from the sun. A white shirt cut very full in the sleeves added an extra touch of the Hollywood buccaneer to his appearance.

"You're trying to save *me* money?" Tarrant was puzzled.

"I don't get. . . . Oh, you're still working on this salinity thing."

"Definitely. I took more samples today. It's up to almost thirty parts per thousand, and that's a gain of three points in the last couple of weeks."

"That's really interesting, Will." Hearing the fervour in the old man's voice, Tarrant began to wish he had not stopped.

Somerville emerged further into view and sat on the edge of the hatchway, his white shirt gleaming in the dusk. "You don't get it, do you, Hal? You don't see the importance of all this."

"Well ... there's a hell of a lot of salt in the sea. I mean, we weren't in danger of running low."

"That's typical!" Somerville threw up his hands in exasperation. "I'm not talking about table salt. I'm talking about the *other* salts, the nitrates and nitrites—the stuff that makes your crop grow."

"Are they on the increase as well?"

"If they remain at the new level we'll all be able to thin out our nutrient sprays by about ten percent. I tell you, Hal, the sea is changing."

Tarrant nodded, unimpressed, and turned to move on. "Keep up the good work."

"What do you care?" Somerville sounded genuinely bitter. "It's just a job to you youngsters, isn't it? It doesn't really matter to you if ... Is that a rifle you've got there?"

"Yes." Tarrant was now certain he should not have stopped.

"Are you going to shoot something?"

"No, I'm going to paddle the boat with it." Tarrant turned to walk away, but Somerville scrambled up on to the jetty with surprising agility and caught his arm.

"Listen, Hal, are you still sticking to this story about somebody sabotaging your booms?"

"It isn't a story," Tarrant said patiently. "When I got out there this morning I found another link undone. God knows how much soup I lost."

"An old bottle-nose must have got tangled up with it."

"Three nights in a row? I'm not buying that one, Will.

19

How many of the other farmers have had dolphin trouble even once?"

"I don't know," Somerville replied, "but there's one thing I can tell you—they don't like you talking about sabotage. Some of us have been here twenty years and more, and we've always worked together."

"Yeah, it's a nice little club here in the inner sectors, but I'm on the outside." Tarrant kept his voice low and even. "I'll farm my spread by myself, and if I find anybody messing around with my booms I'll deal with them by myself. You can pass the word along."

"I still don't see any need for guns," Somerville grumbled. "It doesn't seem right."

Tarrant gently detached the other man's hand from his arm. "Will, I'm going to scare off a few dolphins. Okay?"

"I suppose you're entitled to do that much." Somerville looked undecided. "I'm sorry you've been having trouble—would you like me to ride out with you? Keep you company?"

"No, but thanks." Tarrant smiled, feeling grateful for the offer. "This could be an all-night job."

He walked along the uneven planks of the jetty to his own berth and climbed down into the waiting boat, which was much smaller than Somerville's comfortable cruiser. It took him only a short time to fold the solar energy panels down into their night-time stowage positions and to check the state of his batteries. Satisfied that the boat was seaworthy, he cast off and selected low forward speed. Impelled by silent electric motors, the docile little vessel made its way north past the other farm boats, whose masts were black brush-strokes on the banded copper of the western sky. Tarrant stood in the kiosk-like control house and steered across the broad stretch of open water which separated the inner algae beds from the shore. Two beacons marked the entrance to the main north-wards channel. As soon as the boat had passed between them into the ultra-calm water of the channel he advanced the speed-control lever and settled down for the hour-long journey to the outer sectors of the farm.

Tarrant was a comparative newcomer to the Cawley Island farm and, in consequence, had been allocated one of the rim sectors. Its principal disadvantage was that it required him to schedule two hours of his working day for travelling—and four hours if he had to make a mid-shift return to the island—but this was something he accepted without any complaint. He had previously spent six years in the armed forces of the kingdom of South Newzealand, and had been unlucky enough to be an interceptor pilot during the period when the ruler was refusing to accept the fact that he could no longer maintain an air force.

There had been little menace from outside, because the various would-be warlords of Melanesia—defeated by distance and dwindling technical resources—lapsed into prehistoric silence. The real threat to Tarrant's life had lain in the aircraft he was obliged to fly. Most of them had been copies of copies of copies, dangerous offspring of flawed messenger chains, and only the purest good fortune had enabled him to survive several crashes.

Like most other young airmen, Tarrant had been convinced of his own immortality, but when the prestige-conscious king had instituted a space programme—based on century-old ion-riders—he had begun to have doubts. After several training excursions in a space craft, in which some of the flight instruments were marked in German and others in Spanish, he had decided to find safer employment. It was not permitted for expensively groomed pilot officers to resign from the Air Force, so he had booked ten days' leave, bought a trustworthy boat and sailed off into the north-east. That had been three years earlier, but he still found a sense of peaceful luxury in slow-speed water travel.

By the time Tarrant was halfway out to the rim of the farm all traces of sunlight had fled from the western horizon and he was steering between strings of dim marker lights. The booms which constrained the algae beds were in the form of inflated double tubes. To facilitate maintenance and repair they were in thirty-metre sections, and at the top of each joint was a small glowball powered by a cell which used the sea as an electrolyte. The glowballs guided Tarrant's way as he sailed northwards, but he knew he could have managed almost as well by the light of the stars. They shone brilliantly overhead, seemingly close at hand, turning the night sky into an incredible cityscape. Tarrant had no difficulty in seeing each of them as a sun in its own right, and he experienced a pang of regret that man had proved unequal to the challenges of interstellar flight.

Philosophical considerations faded from his mind as the boundary of his own sector came into view. He switched off all lights on the boat, trimmed it for quiet, slow running, and began a stealthy patrol of the booms. Gliding along in the green-scented darkness, with the stillness of the ocean all around, he almost immediately began to question the wisdom of what he was doing. During the day he had been certain he was right, but now his reasoning seemed at fault. Anybody who wanted to make trouble for him, and was prepared to sail out this far at night to do it, could have made much better use of his time by slashing a few booms. The unlinking of two sections was a comparatively minor annoyance, more on the level of an adolescent prank, and one simply did not find mischievous juveniles roaming the ocean in the darkness.

As Tarrant continued his slow progress to the north he recalled what Will Somerville had said about dolphins, and the idea that they were responsible began to seem increasingly reasonable. Dolphins were very intelligent, possessed of a strong sense of curiosity, and they were notorious for having a misplaced sense of fun. Tarrant had never heard of them interfering with farm equipment before, but it occurred to him that he ought to have spent that day wiring his boom connectors in such a way that they could be opened only with cutters. He gnawed his lower lip for a moment then decided that, as he had come out so far, he might as well make one circuit of the sector before heading back to the shore.

Now feeling slightly self-conscious, Tarrant increased the boat's speed a little and began estimating how long it would take him to return home. He had told Beth he would not be calling on her that night, but—provided he did not arrive too late—her mother might allow him to have coffee with the family. The extra visit would help establish his credentials as a suitor and bring closer the time when Beth and he would be allowed unchaperoned meetings. He allowed his thoughts to dwell on the heady prospect of some day being alone with Beth, eventually in the secure privacy of a bed-room.... All at once, his furtive night patrol seemed totally ridiculous. He was close to the northern edge of his sector and, seeing the open water ahead, he stepped up the boat's speed again and swung in a wide curve to the east. His hand was moving towards the switch of the navigation lights when he detected a curious movement a short distance along the northern boom.

The glowball on the fifth connector was bobbing up and down in a way that had nothing to do with the action of the waves. And as he focussed his gaze on the dim light he saw it being momentarily blotted out, as if a body had passed in front of it.

Tarrant immediately cut his motor and let the boat continue its gradual turn on momentum only. He picked up the rifle, turned his spot-light towards the clandestine activity, and waited for the boat's residual energy to bring him close to the boom. During this silent approach he heard a harsh chirping, unlike any human or animal sound he knew, which came from the direction of the connector. He flexed his neck muscles, trying to dispel a growing sense of unease, and waited until the boat had described a semicircle and was nuzzling against the boom on the opposite side of the disturbance. When it was at rest, giving him a fairly reliable platform, he switched on the big light.

He got an instantaneous vision of three masses of brownish tentacles sprawled over the inflation tubes of the boom. In the centre of each mass a yellowish, plate-sized eye rolled frantically for a moment, then steadied in his direction.

Tarrant was unable to repress a tremulous sigh of fear. He

was not a man of the sea, had no affinity with its inhabitants, and to him the creatures in the spotlight's beam were embodiments of pure dread.

Long seconds dragged by before his mind recovered from the numbing impact and allowed him to make some assessment of what he saw. The creatures were large, far more massive than a man, and his first impression was that they had to be octopuses—then he noticed the rigid, conical bodies sloping down into the water. He knew this to be characteristic of the common squid, but he had never heard of them growing to such frightening size.

So great was Tarrant's revulsion that he felt it had to be mutual, that the creatures were therefore bound either to attack or flee. Instead—after a sombre, speculative stare—they turned their eyes away from him and their tentacles writhed over the boom connectors, almost as if they were deliberately trying to slip the plastic pins. The combined weight of their bodies flattened the boom tubes and allowed the enriched algae soup to spill into the outer water. Apparently this activity had been going on for some time because the surface was stained green for as far as Tarrant could see. The water itself was strangely agitated, and a closer look showed him that the area was alive with fish attracted by the rich planktonic food which had been poured into it.

While Tarrant watched, two thick tentacles broke through the surface and sank out of sight again, and he knew there were other squid down below, feeding on the fish. The discovery increased his alarm, because it suggested that the monsters were intelligent. They appeared to be acting in concert—some of them spilling bait into the water, while others fed.

Tarrant swore silently and raised the rifle to his shoulder. The light was not good for shooting, but the range was only a few metres and he knew he was not going to miss.

He aimed at the nearest of the three creatures on the boom and squeezed the trigger. The rifle punched back into his shoulder and in the same instant the squid's huge eye exploded. The creature gave a shrill cry, its tentacles straightened out, quivering, and the glistening brown body slipped down into the water. Both the remaining squid froze into immobility, draped across the boom, their eyes fixed on him with a kind of mournful expectancy. Tarrant, who had anticipated that they would vanish with his first shot, lined up on the nearest and fired again. It fountained black fluid, but remained in place, seemingly defying him to do his worst.

Appalled by this new evidence of the creatures' alienness, he aimed more carefully at the eye which regarded him from the base of the clustered tentacles. He was tightening his finger on the trigger when there was a raucous, bird-like chirp from somewhere to his right and both squid dropped down into the water. Greenish whorls of algae marked the points where they had disappeared.

Tarrant swung the spotlight around, splashing light over the general area from which the sound had come, but there was nothing to be seen except for the patterns of ripples caused by the feeding fish. He remained still for a moment, then decided to go closer to the boom connector and see if he could find the body of the squid he thought he had fatally injured. People on shore were not going to believe his story unless he had evidence to back it up. He moved the speed control forward a little and the boat began to edge forward, but it felt strangely heavy. Concerned at the idea of being stranded in such circumstances, Tarrant switched on all his lights and inspected the various meters on the control panel. Everything in the power system appeared to be in perfect working order, and yet the boat was sluggish. The next step was to see if anything was fouling the propeller.

Switching off the power, he hung the rifle up by its strap and turned away from the controls to go aft. He had taken one pace when the deck tilted away beneath him and he fell to the side of the boat. A second later the craft rocked in the other direction and he had to catch a stanchion to avoid sliding towards the opposite bulwark. At once the deck rotated again, more violently, until the gunwale beside Tarrant was almost under water; then the swing was reversed. It was obvious to him that the boat was going to capsize unless he did something to prevent the wild oscillations, but as yet he had no clear idea of what was causing them.

Clinging tightly to the stanchion with one hand, he reached for the top of the gunwale with the other in an effort to regain his feet. His hand encountered a curving, leathery object which he took to be a lifebelt until he glanced towards it and saw the mottled grey-and-brown skin and rows of whitish suckers. He had grasped the end of a tentacle belonging to a squid which was clinging to the underside of the boat.

Tarrant let go at once, just as the deck dropped away again, and he fell against the single midship mast. He threw his arms around it and tried to line himself up for a dive into the cockpit where he had left the rifle. From the corners of his eyes he saw the movement of tentacles at several points along the gunwales. The squid was consolidating its hold.

The deck rotated sickeningly once more and, trying to judge the mid-point of the sweep, Tarrant threw himself forward. His shoulder collided painfully with a doorpost, but he tumbled into the cockpit and was able to wedge himself in the confined area. His first thought was for the rifle, and he was unutterably thankful to find it swinging from the hook on which he had placed it. He caught hold of the weapon and pointed it at the deck.

From the spread of its tentacles and the way it was able to affect the boat, he guessed the squid was even larger than those he had seen, but there was no time to try working out where best to place his shots. At the limit of its last gyration the deck was almost vertical and had Tarrant not been braced against the cockpit housing he would have gone overboard. He worked the rifle's trigger and the high-velocity bullets snapped a series of almost invisible holes in the wood of the deck. They seemed totally inadequate compared with the bulk of the squid, but Tarrant was counting on the slugs deforming and exiting through the boat's plastic bottom as spinning, ragged cutting implements.

Somewhere around his seventh or eight shot he felt a shudder go through the boat, the tips of the tentacles vanished from the gunwales, and the oscillations abruptly damped down. The spotlight was pointing towards the water and Tarrant caught one glimpse of a vast, conical body followed by an intent, rueful eye and a thrashing of tentacles as the squid torpedoed away in the direction of the open sea. Within a second there was nothing visible but slow-swirling algae.

Tarrant slumped back against the steering column, breathing heavily, then he noticed that the shallow bilge space had already filled and that water was welling up through the bullet holes in the deck. He gathered up some empty cartridge cases and jammed their narrow necks into the holes, effecting a temporary seal. When he switched on the motor the boat still felt sluggish, because of the water it had shipped, but he was confident it would get him back to the shore—provided that nothing extraordinary happened.

He brought the little craft round into the main radial channel, selected maximum forward speed, and tried to make himself relax as he rode south through the watchful darkness.

# CHAPTER THREE

The light grew stronger as they neared the surface of the world, and Myrah had to narrow her eyes to screen out the excessive brilliance. Even in her mood of detachment, she was intrigued, as always, at the way in which her skin and that of the other swimmers began to show colour changes with the increase in brightness. Her fingertips developed tinges of red and her nipples slowly altered from near-black to a pinkish brown. As the livid quality faded from the bodies of the others she noticed that lips were now pink instead of blue, that fair hair was shining like newly-cut brass, and that even the swimmers' eyes displayed variations in shade.

The idea crossed Myrah's mind, not for the first time, that it was curiously wasteful for human beings to possess colour attributes which were not visible in their normal environment at the level of the Home. To her this seemed almost an indication that humans were meant to live close to the surface, although her logic was defeated by the daily temperature variations which made the uppermost levels of the world unsuitable for habitation.

The ice sheet was close above her now, and she could feel chill currents brushing across her skin. A canopy of green leaves spread out through the ice from the top of the root column, and in the distances opened up to her vision by the brilliance she could see similar giant plants, hugely motionless, forming a backdrop to the immediate scene. The other members of the group, all swimming separately now, were unfolding their bags of watertight skin and slowly paddling upwards with spears at the ready. In between the areas of foliage the surface shone with an intolerable cloudy brilliance which gave the drifting air bubbles the appearance of solid globes of silver, and made the fish darting through them glitter like multi-hued jewels.

Braving the coldness of the water, Myrah swam close to the ice and began chipping out a large section with her spear. The ice was thicker than usual because they had arrived at the surface so early in the day, and she had to work hard to cut through to the emptiness beyond. Finally the section came free, opening an irregular window to the outside, and Myrah saw the white fire of the sun burning through the encircling mist. Air bubbles crowded past her, elongating as they disappeared into the void, and she kept her head well back to reduce the risk of losing the bubble from her cage.

She drew the bag over the transparent block, being careful to exclude salt water, and sealed it by pressing the mastic-coated edges together. As soon as she had secured her quota of ice, Myrah swam down into warmer waters and waited for the rest of the group to reassemble. She was not timid by nature, but every member of the Clan knew about the strange death which awaited those who were incautious enough to let themselves be carried outside. It was said that their faces turned black as they floated away in the mist, and that— even though they were obviously screaming in agony—no sound emerged from their mouths. This was evidence enough for Myrah that the surface of the world was, in fact, the edge of an alien universe, and even the prospect of someday drifting down into Ka's dark fronds was preferable to the thought of being suspended for ever in the sterile white loneliness outside.

Geean approached Myrah with her ice bag in tow, her hair glinting oddly red in the plentiful light. She paused to trap a bubble and said, "Give me your bag, Myrah."

Myrah shook her head. "I'll take it back."

"But you came up alone—you're entitled to swim back with one of the men."

"I'm going alone, thanks."

"Well ... can I have your place?"

"You're welcome to it." Myrah spoke with a show of disinterest.

Geean smiled uncertainly. She was barely sixteen and had a fragile slimness of form which suggested to Myrah that she would begin to cough at an early age. "Don't you want your chance, Myrah? It might be a long time before you're on another ice trip."

"I'm not superstitious," Myrah said curtly.

"It isn't a superstition." Geean looked hurt. "Everybody knows that God makes women more fertile while they gather water for drinking. It's been proved."

"How do you know it isn't something to do with our being midway between periods when we go for ice?"

"What do you mean?"

"Nothing." Myrah looked at the pinched, pretty face and was immediately sorry she had tried to weaken any structure of faith which was helping Geean through what was likely to be a short existence.

"Why don't you give me your bag and start getting yourself a partner?" She smiled and held out her hand. "We'll be going back soon."

"Thanks, Myrah." Geean squeezed her hand in gratitude while she was transferring the bag, and then darted away through the shimmering brilliance with the agility of an elver. Myrah attached the thongs of the two bags to her belt and cruised in a small circle while looking for delicacies which might be available near the surface. There was no food visible, but she found a clump of stingweed growing on a branch. It was a tough material which contracted violently when removed from contact with the water, and it was used to power the Home's air pumps.

By the time she had cut the clump free and put it in a carrying net the other members of the group were ready for the return journey. Young Geean, looking pleased with herself, had managed to pair off with Lennar. Myrah, Caro, and the other two females who had been with men on the way up formed an outer ring. Lennar stared at Myrah for a moment,

30

obviously wondering why she had surrendered her rightful place in the centre of the formation, but voicing any query would have implied a rejection of Geean and she knew he would not do that. He gave the signal to descend and the group swam downwards, away from the light.

Myrah had been swimming only a short time when she became aware of Caro approaching from the left. Caro closed in until their bodies were touching and merged their bubbles with an abrupt forward movement of her head.

"Why did you do it?" she whispered.

"Do what?"

"You know what I mean. Geean couldn't make a child if she lived to be fifty." Caro's face was taut with anger and the filigreed petals of her bubble cage clicked against Myrah's.

"Get back to your station," Myrah said quietly. "You're supposed to be on guard."

"Nothing ever happens up here and you know it. You're jealous of me, aren't you?"

Myrah gripped her shoulder. "If you don't get back to your station I'll report you to the Council—and you won't gather ice again until you're too old for it to make any difference." She pushed Caro away with a powerful thrust which spun both of their bodies.

Caro's air bubble broke up into a flurry of tiny spheres and she had to swim a few strokes to one side to pick up a fresh one. She turned back to Myrah, intent on continuing the quarrel, and failed to see the dark brown shape darting towards her from a deep crevice in the nearby root columns.

"Behind you!" Myrah screamed, and from the corner of her eye she saw the couples in the centre of the circle break away from each other.

Caro froze for a fatal instant, her mouth wide open with shock, before twisting round to level her spear. The Horra grazed past her in a characteristic attack and its major tentacles, trailing behind the conical body, snaked around Caro, pinning her arms to her sides. She was upside down in relation to the Horra, and Myrah caught a glimpse of the ghastly organic spear of its sexual arm stabbing upwards into Caro's throat. Caro's body convulsed and suddenly the water all around was stained with arterial blood. The Horra, with its propulsion siphon jetting spasmodically, circled back towards its hiding place. Its course took it near the centre of the group and one of the men, Toms, lunged at it with his spear. The sharpened tube entered its mantle cavity, just behind one of the eyes. The Horra shrilled in pain, but was not slowed down.

With Caro's body clutched against its central mouth, it continued its pulsating flight towards the root column, the two ice bags which Caro had been carrying spinning in its wake. It reached the vertical cleft and writhed inside, using the longest of its ten tentacles to give it purchase. Toms was close behind the Horra, and Myrah saw him grasp the protruding end of his spear and try to drive it further into the unseen shape. Without any fixed point to provide leverage, his limbs threshed water ineffectually as though he too had been wounded.

"Come back," Lennar shouted to him. "There's nothing you can do, Toms."

"I can kill it." Toms' voice was cracked and distorted by the commotion in the water. "I'm going to kill it."

Lennar signalled the rest of the group to continue moving downwards. "There's no need, Toms—look around you."

Toms steadied himself in the water and his face altered, the instinct for self-preservation returning, as he became aware of the amount of blood which was hazing his immediate area. He backed off immediately and swam downwards just as the first flecks of silver-blue light came speeding out of nowhere. The ripperfish were as small as a woman's finger, but so voracious that even one of them could inflict serious wounds on an adult human. Normally unobtrusive, they appeared so quickly on the scent of blood that in Clan legend they were reputed to materialise from the water itself. Within the space of a few breaths the slow-curling billows of redness issuing from the Horra's lair were obliterated by blankets of silver needles. Toms came swimming down to the comparative safety of the level where the group had assembled, his eyes wide with shock.

"I can't believe it," he said. "A Horra! What was a Horra doing so near the surface?"

One of the other men handed him the spear which Caro had failed to use. "It might be something to do with the new current again, or perhaps they live on the surface in other parts of the world."

"I don't think so," Lennar said. "If they were used to moving in ripperfish territory they'd know not to take any food they couldn't swallow whole."

"That one will have learned its mistake by this time."

"Stop it! *Stop it!*" Geean's limbs were rigid and quivering with hysteria. "Caro wasn't *food.*"

"She was," Lennar said firmly. "As soon as you stop keeping guard you turn yourself into a piece of food. It's the first rule."

Geean turned to him, her small face contorted with grief. "Rules! How can you talk like that when you'd just swum with her. She was carrying your rotten seed when it happened."

"Personal feelings don't change the rules," Lennar said, his voice harsh. He broke away to capture an air bubble, then came back to Myrah, spreading his hands to check his forward movement. "I saw Caro with you. Why did she leave her station?"

Myrah glanced at Geean and guessed she was not ready to hear what Caro had been saying. "She thought the seal on one of my ice bags was opening up."

"Not a good enough reason to go off guard. What did you say to her about it?"

"I told her to get back in formation."

Lennar gave Myrah a thoughtful stare. "At least I'll be able to report to the Council that somebody did something right."

"I want to go home," Geean said in a quavering voice. Her face was blank, the eyes flat and lifeless.

33

Lennar shook his head. "Not just yet—we can't afford to leave Toms' spear."

Myrah followed his gaze upward and saw that the swarm of ripperfish had already begun to thin out, its food supply almost exhausted. In a few moments all the small glittering bodies had vanished. Lennar swam up to the crevice and looked inside. Myrah knew he would see nothing but one human skeleton and the single pen-shaped, subcutaneous shell which would be all that remained of the Horra. He put his arm into the lair, withdrew a spear and swam back to the group, collecting Caro's slowly tumbling ice bags on the way. His face, behind the reflective veil of his air bubble, showed no trace of emotion, but to Myrah's eyes he seemed older than at the start of the trip.

There was little conversation during the return to the bottom of the euphotic zone. The members of the group swam separately, but in close formation, one of the men adopting a feet-first attitude so that he could scan the water above and behind them. It had never been known for any of the Horra to approach the surface before, but if it had happened once it could happen again and, as the leader of the group, Lennar did not want to take unnecessary risks. Myrah found herself wondering if the loss of Caro would affect the long-established mating rituals of the ice-gathering swims. It was hard to accept that a custom so central to the Clan's way of life might have to be abandoned, but her mind kept returning to a remark Lennar had made early in the day.

*The world seems to be changing*, he had said. At that time, still fresh from her night's sleep, Myrah had been scornful—now she was filled with a gloomy certainty that he had been right.

The Home was a scene of unusual activity when they descended on it out of the silent blue waters.

Everywhere that Myrah looked on the vast, amorphous structure she glimpsed the figures of men and women either carrying ropes from one point to another, or busy rein-

34

forcing the anchorages of the outer defensive mesh. In those places where the dark shapes of houses projected through the mesh they were criss-crossed with new lines, like whales which were being prevented from making ponderous escapes.

Myrah was disturbed by what she saw. With the almost complete lack of gravity it was easy to secure an edifice as large as the Home, its various attachments to the root columns being used principally to prevent the inner air net from deforming under the action of stray currents. Now, however, it seemed that the Home was being reinforced to withstand an abnormally powerful attack from outside. Myrah turned her head, taking a general view of her environment, and became aware of the fact that the endless shoals of air bubbles, upon which her people depended for their lives, were drifting downwards at a more noticeable rate than had been the case in the morning. Her sense of being threatened grew stronger.

They reached the smaller netted bubble which surrounded the Topeast entrance and went into it one by one. Old Shire, who was back on sentry duty, urged them through with excited gestures which made Myrah resolve not to betray her own fears. She manoeuvred her position so as to be the last of the group to go inside and paused by Shire. The skin bags she was transporting, their contents now melted down into water, surged against her legs as she stopped.

"Keep moving," Shire commanded impatiently.

"What's going on?"

"Solman has called a Clan meeting."

"Why? What happened?"

"The Home has shifted and ..." Shire paused, scowling, suddenly aware he was weakening his new-found authority. "It isn't for the likes of you or me to question the Council, is it?"

Myrah shrugged, handed him her spear and went through to the protected inner waters of the Home. Four strokes took her to the nearest opening in the interior net and she passed through its clinging folds into the giant, artificially maintained bubble in which the people of the Clan spent most of their lives. She took off her bubble cage, closed up its leaves like a fan, and hooked it into her belt. Adapting easily to the change of environment, she propelled herself through the air in a series of gentle flights from guide rope to guide rope, eventually arriving at the dark oval mouth of the water store. The custodian, Jule—a fat woman whose eyes were featureless milky orbs—accepted the water bags from her with a fixed smile. She steered the bulging skins into a net which held others brought in by the group.

"Thank you, Myrah love," she said. "Had a good trip?"

"No. Didn't they tell you? We lost Caro."

"A pity." Jule's smile faded, but was quickly renewed. "Razorfin? Shark?"

"Horra."

"Up at the surface?"

"It might have been lost," Myrah said sarcastically. She was as familiar with premature and violent death as any member of the Clan, but she disliked the blind woman's casual acceptance of the news about Caro. Deciding to change the subject, she glanced around the interior of the water store. It had been chosen for its purpose because, unlike other houses in the Home, it was small and constructed of a whitish metal which seemed immune to serious corrosion. The metal was much thinner than in the bigger houses and its reinforcing ribs were pierced with large circular holes, presumably for decoration.

"I'd love to know where this house came from," Myrah said, touching a sawn edge of metal which protruded from the mastic which held the net in place around the entrance.

"The Clan fathers built it."

"Why?"

"To store water, of course."

Myrah considered asking Jule why a water store should have three large fin-like extrusions at its closed end, then decided there was little point. Jule was quite capable of saying that a house which enabled humans to live in water like fish *ought* to be shaped like a fish. She had lost her sight many years earlier in an encounter with a cumberfish, an immobile species which defended itself by explosive evisceration of its own body when it felt menaced. Usually this resulted in no more than a scare for the swimmer concerned, but the cumberfish had been in a poisonous condition and Jule had contracted an eye disease. Since then she had survived by being optimistic about everything, and Myrah had no wish to infect her with her own mood of depression.

Looking outside the house she saw a fairly steady stream of people flying down into the central region and guessed the Clan meeting was about to start. She said goodbye to Jule and propelled herself from the lip of the water store entrance and slanted down through the webs of rope, suddenly aware that she had had no food since the previous day. There was still time to go to the Artisan family house and pick up a tablet of dried fish—large meetings were always difficult to organise—but her curiosity about what Solman was going to say was too strong. She continued her downward flight to where the Clan had assembled in the largest open space, ranged along guide ropes like complicated beads.

There were less than two hundred of them, and yet this was the total strength of the Clan, excluding infants and the few adults who were engaged on essential work such as guarding the entrances. Myrah had often heard that there had been many more Humans in the Home in the old days, but it saddened her to realise that, even were their numbers to be doubled or trebled, the people of the Clan would still be as nothing compared to the teeming life forms beyond the nets. It seemed to her that their status in the order of things was not merely insignificant, but that it was dangerously close to not existing at all. They were dependent on the fine balance of too many forces; their resources were dwindling to the point at which a single disaster could be sufficient to wipe them out altogether.

And, for all she knew, the final tragedy had already begun. The new current, the disappearance of the best edible fish from their usual feeding grounds, Horra spreading upwards from their dark domain to the surface of the world—all of these could be portents. . . .

"I'd like to know what's wrong with you today," Lennar said, coming down from behind her and grasping the same rope. He caught her belt with his hand and drew their bodies into momentary contact with a courtesy which was at variance with the terseness of his voice.

"Perhaps I don't like seeing people being eaten," Myrah replied without looking at him.

"It started before that."

"I. . . ." Myrah turned reluctantly to face him. "I think I'm afraid, Lennar. I can't see the Clan going on like this for much longer."

"Is that all? I thought it was something serious."

"I'm serious, Lennar."

He pushed his wet black hair away from his forehead and droplets of water slowly swam away in the air, twinkling like minnows. "I told you I don't think about that kind of thing— but if the Clan has always been here why should it suddenly come to an end."

"Has it always been here?"

"Where else is there? Be logical, Myrah." Lennar smiled at her and gave a gentle, tentative thrust with his pelvis. She responded automatically, comforted by his practicality and strength, then her attention was distracted by a low murmur from the assembly as Solman appeared at the entrance to the house of the Council. He was by far the oldest member of the Clan—thought by some to have reached the age of fifty—and the remaining wisps of his hair had turned fish-belly white. Arthritis, which was so common among elders, had restricted the mobility of his limbs to the extent that he rarely was able to enter the water, but he could still fly accurately in air, with a kind of rigid majesty which was somehow in keeping with his position of authority. Circular blue scars patterned his body, proclaiming a veteran of many battles against the Horra.

Myrah watched him with interest, and a perverse flicker

38

of pleasure. She had long been of the opinion that the Clan's leader should concern himself with broader issues than the daily work schedules and the other endless petty details of Home life which appeared to occupy all of Solman's thoughts. Unable to pursue his own activities, he used his power to control the lives of his people in dozens of different and irksome ways. He had, for example, instituted the procedure under which no woman was allowed to pass beyond the defensive mesh without the tally from her House Mother. Myrah regarded the system as both a denial of her individual liberty and an insult to her intelligence. Now, however, Solman was faced with a situation which was a genuine test of leadership, and she was eager to see how he would cope with it. Solman raised his hands to bring silence to the assembly.

"This should be interesting," Myrah whispered.

"Let him speak before you judge," Lennar said.

"He's only going to...." She broke off as Lennar tightened his grip on her belt and twisted it warningly.

"My children," Solman began in a hoarse voice which scarcely reached the outer circles of his audience, "by this time you will all be aware that we, as a people, are faced with a problem which is unprecedented in our history. The steady downward transfer of water which began twelve days ago has now...."

He paused to allow an audible ripple of surprise to die away. "I know that the existence of the current became obvious only three days ago when its speed began to build up, but it was detected some time earlier. The Council decided against making any announcement or taking any precipitate action until we were certain that the current was not merely a freakish—but nonetheless natural—phenomenon which would eventually correct itself.

"Today, as you know, it became necessary to strengthen all the anchorages of the Home to prevent movement of the houses and nets ... and it is my duty now to inform you that, in the opinion of the Council, we are facing a major crisis. The speed of the current increases slightly each day as it establishes itself. We do not know how long this process will continue, but even if we could reinforce the Home to withstand it, there is the inescapable fact that it will eventually rob us of our air supplies.

"The Council have debated the problem for many hours, and we have chosen a course of action. I will not pretend to you that we are sure our choice is the correct one, or that it will necessarily end the threat to the Home. All I can tell you is that it is the only positive plan we can conceive, and that—to implement it—some of you will be called upon to display the ultimate degree of courage."

There was an immediate uproar which prevented Solman from continuing, and a visible wave of agitation swept through the hemispherical cluster of men and women he was facing. Myrah had listened to his words with a growing sense of astonishment. This was not the fussy, trivialising Solman she had previously encountered in the day-to-day life of the Home. His face was grave and yet calm, and the formality of his speech—with liberal use of terms whose meaning she had to guess from context—had created in her mind a new impression of him, a semblance of one of the mysterious and dignified king-figures of her childhood. It came to her that all along she might have been too superficial and facile with her estimates of Solman's character and worth. The realisation brought with it a feeling of shame mingled with pleasure over the discovery that the Clan's leaders were more capable than she had supposed.

*Is it possible*, she wondered, newly hopeful, *that they know what to do?*

Solman raised his hands again, commanding silence. "We are almost certain," he said, "that the new current is not one of the natural mechanisms by which the world adjusts to temperature changes, and that its motive force must lie close to the centre of the world."

There was a second commotion among his audience, and this time Myrah detected an undertow of fear, a sinking of the communal spirit. Her skin prickled coldly as she began

40

to have premonitions about what was coming next.

"We have a number of choices," Solman continued. "We could cut the Home free, before it is destroyed, and perhaps go with it wherever the current takes us. We could abandon the Home, and take one or two houses to another, safer location where we can begin rebuilding. Or we could decide to fight the current and keep on strengthening our ties and anchorages.

"But if we can act at all in this matter, it can only be on the basis of definite knowledge. If we can act at all, it cannot be done at a distance. The Council is therefore asking for six volunteers who are prepared to follow the new current as far into the darkness as it will take them."

Paradoxically, Myrah's first reaction was one of relief. Ka was waiting at the heart of the world, and it suddenly came to her that, no matter how unsatisfactory her life might be, she was immeasurably better off than any of the six who would journey down to meet him. It was good, marvellously good, to know that—while they were sinking, heroically but so foolishly, into death's domain—she would sleep in the security of the Home. She looked around her, luxuriating in the warm sense of being one of the crowd, curious to see which of the others would be sufficiently vainglorious, sufficiently suicidal, to go forward.

Her whole body stiffened with shock as, before she could move to prevent him, Lennar cast off from beside her. He flew downwards in silence, through the sad blue light, and was caught and steadied by Solman's right hand. Myrah saw Solman whisper something to Lennar before embracing him.

*Insufficient reward*, she thought. *That's not enough.*

There was a flicker of movement to her left as another member of the Clan went forward, a woman named Treece who had always been something of an enigma to Myrah. In the distance she saw a man beginning to move, but her attention was distracted by an event closer at hand. Myrah shook her head in disbelief as she identified the pale, slim form of young Geean, the immature girl who had been overwhelmed by the sight of one unremarkable death only a short time earlier. Geean's flight took her straight to Lennar, and Myrah began to wonder if there was some kind of emotional fixation involved. If there was she might have contributed to it by bringing Geean and Lennar together during the morning's swim.

"This is madness," she said aloud, launching herself free of the guide rope. During the first few moments of her flight she was almost able to believe she was moving to intercept Geean, but then—as Solman's arms spread to receive her— she understood that only by surrendering her life had she any hope of giving it real meaning.

# CHAPTER FOUR

Tarrant knew his boat was likely to sink during the night if he tied it up at the jetty. He ran it on past the line of farm craft, hearing them creak and jostle each other as his wash brought them briefly out of their sleep, and kept going until he grounded on the beach.

The sea front was in darkness, the widely separated standard lamps serving only to mark the line of the narrow road which followed the upper edge of the sand. Localised brightness from the pearly globes had the effect of neutralising the starlight. Tarrant found himself strangely reluctant to jump into the black water, even where it was less than a metre in depth, but it was obvious he would get no outside help with the job of securing the boat.

He retracted the propeller, threw a coiled mooring rope ahead on to the beach, and jumped off the prow, almost managing to clear the water's edge. Normally he would have been able to drag the light, shallow-draught boat on to dry land, but with its bilge spaces full of water it resisted all his efforts to move it. With some assistance from small waves he got its nose ashore, then compromised by running a long line up to the stump of a palm tree. Satisfied that the boat would remain in place while the tide receded during the night, he collected his rifle and walked towards the vague pyramid of street lights and glowing rectangular windows which was the body of the island.

He was surprised to discover so many households were still awake and then a glance at his watch showed him that, incredibly, it was not yet eleven o'clock. It seemed to Tarrant that much more than three hours had elapsed since he set out to patrol his sector. Now that he was safely back on land, surrounded by the cosy normality of the community and the breath of night-scented flowers, his encounter with the squid was like an unusually vivid nightmare. Frightening though the physical aspect of the monsters had been, the horror which lingered in Tarrant's mind sprang from what he remembered of their behaviour. They had appeared to act in concert, like men, and with an extraordinary degree of intelligence. He had never heard of squid partially leaving the water, as those on the boom had done, and the largest one with the mottled skin trying to capsize his boat was something that was beginning to seem incredible, even to Tarrant. For some reason, recalling the entire episode, he was left with the disturbing impression that he had fought a skirmish with a platoon of enemy soldiers commanded by a tough, experienced sergeant.

The notion produced a cool, crawling sensation between his shoulder blades and he felt a sudden desire to be in the company of other human beings. He increased his stride and walked up the hill in the direction of the Kircher house. Several windows in the building were glowing with ivory light when he arrived, and when he knocked on the door there was an immediate sound of movement within. Cissy Kircher, Beth's mother, opened the door a little and her jaw sagged with surprise.

"Hal!" Her gaze traversed him from head to foot. "What's the matter?"

He smiled. "It's all right, Mrs Kircher—I just wanted to call on Beth. It isn't too late, is it?"

"But you're soaking wet. And what happened to your head? Did you have a fall?"

Tarrant put a hand to his forehead and felt something like flakes of dried paint on the skin. "I'm fine. I'd like to see Beth, if it isn't too late."

Mrs Kircher made no move to admit him. She turned her head and, raising her voice, said, "It's Hal Tarrant, Kenneth. Can you come to the door, please?"

Tarrant began to realise he had made a mistake in coming directly to Beth's home from his boat. Obviously his appearance was not compatible with the image of a respectable, responsible suitor which he had so carefully nurtured in the elder Kirchers' minds. Cissy Kircher, her incongruously voluptuous form wrapped in a tie-belted gown of black murex, continued to examine him suspiciously. Tarrant had never before seen her in anything but formal dress and he guessed she had been preparing for bed. It occurred to him that, even at the age of fifty, she was a well-equipped bedmate. His immediate reaction was one of guilt that he should have thought in that way about Beth's mother. He strove to put the intrusive vision out of his head, but his gaze was drawn back across the light-accentuated contours of her body. At once she closed a fold of material across her throat, and Tarrant came near to panic.

"I expect Mr Kircher will be harvesting soon," he said. Cissy Kircher, undeceived, gave him a tight smile and did not reply.

"Is that Hal?" Kenneth Kircher said jovially, appearing behind her. "Why didn't you bring him in? We're always ..." He stopped speaking and advanced cautiously into the cone of luminance from the porch light as he saw Tarrant. "Is there something wrong, Hal?"

"I called to see Beth. I didn't realize it was so late."

Kircher moved further into the light and his scalp glistened roundly beneath fine strands of hair. He was a plump, healthy-looking man who tanned red rather than brown, and who usually had sun blisters on his lower lip. Narrowing his eyes he said, "Hal, are you carrying a rifle?"

"Yes, Mr Kircher." Tarrant unslung the weapon from his shoulder and stood it in a corner of the porch, dissociating himself from it. "I ran into some trouble out on my sector."

Kircher scanned the darkness behind Tarrant as though concerned about his neighbours seeing him do something of which he was ashamed. "You'd better come in and tell us about it."

Tarrant nodded and followed the Kirchers through the hall and into a long, split-level living room which had a glossy wooden floor and cane furniture with orange-and-rust cushions. In one corner stood an antique console television which had, in place of a picture tube, a brightly lit aquarium set into it. The door to the adjoining kitchen was partially open, showing a table covered with baking requisites. Beth Kircher was seated at the table while she filled pastry cases. She was a black-haired girl in her mid-twenties, with full lips and exceptionally white teeth. She jumped to her feet and hurried into the living room as soon as she saw Tarrant, her face registering surprise and concern. Now aware of the blood on his forehead, Tarrant gave her a reassuring smile.

"I'm all right," he said. "It's not as bad as it looks."

"What happened to you, Hal?" Beth's cheeks were pink with the heat from the oven in the kitchen, and she exuded an aroma of orange peel and spices. Her bosom, a slightly less voluminous and more buoyant model of her mother's, worked against the constraints of a flowered shirt. The ambience of sex and domesticity overwhelmed Tarrant, filling him with a yearning to be married to Beth.

"I was out on my boat tonight and I managed to crack my head on the mast," he said, glancing tentatively at a chair.

"Yes, sit down." Kircher gestured at the chair and sat in the one facing it. "You said there was some trouble at your sector?"

"I'll get a damp sponge for your forehead." Beth went back into the kitchen with a flounce of tautly covered hips.

"I've been a bit worried about some of the things I've been hearing about you, Hal," Kircher continued. "A co-operative farm like ours is more than just a joint business, you know. It's an association—an association of gentlemen, if you like— and any suggestion that one of our members would vandalise another member's equipment simply doesn't go down well." Kircher's red-brown face pleaded with Tarrant to be gentlemanly. "It's all a matter of trust, and if you...."

"I was wrong about that," Tarrant said quickly. "I found

46

out what was causing the damage tonight."

Kircher sat back in his chair and looked pleased. "Worn connectors, was it?"

"Squid. The biggest ones I've ever seen. They were crawling up on my booms."

"Squid?" Kircher glanced worriedly at his wife, who was lowering herself into a nearby chair. "I've often heard of giant squid, Hal, but I've never seen one."

Tarrant had anticipated disbelief, but not so early in his story. "I don't know too much about marine life, but isn't the giant squid a recognised class?"

"As far as I remember it's in the genus *Architeuthis*."

"Well, these weren't *Architeuthis*. They were the same shape as the common squid—I could tell they had pointed shells inside them—but their tentacles were two or three metres long."

Kircher shook his head. "If you're talking about *Loligo*— they never get above half a metre overall."

"Here we are!" Beth emerged from the kitchen carrying a sponge and a basin of water. She set the basin on a small table, moistened the sponge and began to dab Tarrant's forehead with it. He had to part his legs to let her move in close to him and he suddenly found that her breasts, which he had never been allowed to touch in six months of steady courtship, were almost in contact with his face. At once there was an opening of organic sluicegates in his groin. He turned his eyes to one side only to encounter Cissy Kircher's accusing stare.

"Beth," she said firmly, "I think Hal is old enough to do that for himself." She stood up, twitching her gown into place, and picked up the basin. "Come on! We've got to get the kitchen tidied up—I don't see why you had to start baking at this time of night."

"Yes, mother." Smiling ruefully, Beth handed Tarrant the sponge and withdrew into the kitchen, accompanied by her mother.

Tarrant turned back to Kenneth Kircher, who was regarding him with a puzzled expression which suggested he had sensed an undercurrent of feeling in the room without being able to identify it. It would all be explained to him later, Tarrant knew, and his spirits sank as he realised that, far from improving his standing as a suitor, the impromptu visit had seriously worsened his chances of acceptance. He wondered briefly what it must have been like to live in the 20th century, before the population crisis and the subsequent horrors of natural adjustment had ushered in the new morality. Sexual repression was at its greatest in a small, closed community such as that on Cawley Island—especially as there was little access to reliable contraceptives—and there had been times when he had considered packing up and sailing away to one of the continents where standards were less rigid or not so uniformly observed. He had known in his heart, however, that a man who would go to that sort of length in search of physical gratification would have to be some kind of degenerate, and the self-respect instilled by his upbringing had enabled him to weather the emotional squalls.

Kircher gave a low chuckle. "What's the game, Hal? Are you doing a bit of play-acting to impress Beth? It won't work, you know."

"There's no game," Tarrant said doggedly. "I almost got killed tonight." He went on to describe the events at the northern rim of the farm, ending with an account of how he had to blast the bottom out of his boat in order to get away from the underwater attacker. Kircher's expression grew progressively more grave as he listened.

"No disrespect to you, Hal," he said, "but this is kind of hard to take in. Big squid leaving the water to open your booms ... attacking your boat...."

"Would you like to see my boat?" Tarrant tried not to sound aggrieved. "I didn't shoot holes in it for fun."

"Of course you didn't—but it must have been pretty dark out there, and if...."

"If what, Mr Kircher?"

48

"Well...." Kircher gave an embarrassed laugh. "If you'd had a drink."

"I hadn't had a drink." Tarrant knew that Kircher was a teetotaller of the kind who believed that one glass of wine was enough to turn a man into a witless animal. "If you don't count coffee, that is."

"Oh, I'm not suggesting.... Where would beasts like that come from?"

"Could there be a new upwelling current that's bringing them out of the deep?"

"It hardly seems likely. Squid aren't planktonic, you know —they control their own whereabouts in the sea." Kircher seemed relieved to get back on to the neutral subject of marine biology.

"I was talking to Will Somerville before I went out," Tarrant persisted. "He says the composition of the ocean around here is definitely changing."

"What does he know? He's fooling himself if he thinks he's going to get anywhere with all that fiddling about with test tubes." Kircher's berry-coloured face mirrored his pride as he gestured at a shelf of textbooks, all of which had carefully mended covers. "It's all there in the books, Hal. I go by the experts."

"Yes, but those books were written a hundred years ago, or more."

"It doesn't matter." Kircher gave Tarrant a patient smile. "The sea doesn't change."

"But that's exactly the...." It came to Tarrant that he was on the verge of worsening his position with regard to Beth by quarrelling with her father. He sat quietly for a moment, pressing the coolness of the damp sponge to his forehead.

"Perhaps you ought to go home and get to bed," Kircher said. "Why did you want to see me, anyway?"

"Actually, I called to see Beth. I was hoping it wasn't too late in the evening."

"Beth?" Kircher looked at a wallclock and kept his gaze on it long enough to show that he was only noting the time, but wondering how anybody would have the temerity to try visiting a respectable girl late at night in wet clothes, with dried blood on his forehead, and carrying a rifle. "Had you any special reason for wanting to see her?"

"No." *I just want to father children on her*, Tarrant thought bitterly. *But that doesn't count.*

"In that case...." Kircher looked at Tarrant with kindly reproach.

"I guess I wasn't thinking too clearly." Tarrant got to his feet and set the sponge on the table. "I'll take your advice and turn in for the night. Good night, Mr Kircher."

"Good night, Hal."

As they were walking to the door, Tarrant glanced wistfully towards the kitchen, hoping that Beth would appear and assert some degree of independence by speaking to him, if only for a few seconds. She remained out of sight, and almost before he knew what was happening he found himself outside in the darkness, alone and defeated, walking up the hill to his house.

When he got indoors he spent ten minutes cleaning the rifle, then sat down at his window seat with a bottle of home-made coconut wine. The pale liquor seemed too bland and cloying, however, and he was unable to work up any interest in any of the half-dozen books he had partially read. Because of the blackness beyond, the window acted as a mirror, presenting him with the evidence of his solitude and thereby emphasising it. He had several spells of fantasising about Beth, but this produced an emotional torture so intense that, paradoxically, there would have been no point in self-relief. His mind as well as his body needed to share in the rituals of love, and as he stared out to sea—trying to peer through his own reflection—he thought again about provisioning his boat and sailing off towards Asia or the Americas. Changes might be taking place in the unseen ocean, but it seemed that nothing would ever alter the rigid social customs of Cawley Island.

# CHAPTER FIVE

As a member of the Artisan family, Myrah was given responsibility for the habitat in which the volunteers would sleep.

It was basically an air net which was roomy enough to contain several humans, and its mechanical components consisted of two pumps and a large collapsible cage for the trapping of free air bubbles. The pumps themselves were cylindrical devices with a system of valves which allowed water to be expelled alternately from each side of a piston. Bands of stringweed were attached to both faces of the piston. As soon as one strip of weed was deprived of water it contracted powerfully, causing the piston to move under its action and, at the limit of its travel, water was admitted to that section of the cylinder. The stringweed then relaxed, just as the opposing band was drying and contracting, and the piston was drawn to the other end of its stroke. Although slow in operation, pumps of this type were reliable and efficient at maintaining a slight positive air pressure in the Home's various living spaces.

The portable habitat was designed to allow small groups of humans to sleep in a reasonable degree of security while away from the Home on long journeys. One of its pumps was an air intake and the other, positioned at the opposite side of the net, expelled the air again at a slightly lesser rate. This arrangement resulted in sufficient air pressure to keep the net inflated, and also created an air flow which ensured that the people within did not asphyxiate in their sleep. In the virtual absence of gravity there was no convection to carry warm, used air away from a sleeper, and one of the most common dangers facing a human was that of falling asleep in a zone of still air and being smothered in a cloud of his own exhalations.

Myrah slept very badly on the night before departure.

She had purposely worked until she was very tired, hoping to induce swift unconsciousness, but the enormity of what was going to happen in the morning was too great. Time and time again she drifted into uneasy dozes, only to dream about tumbling downwards into the darkness where Ka was waiting. When she awoke there was momentary relief at having escaped from the nightmare, then came the pounding realisation that the nightmare had become reality and that it had scarcely yet begun. In the end she was almost glad to see that morning had come, because it meant that the events of the dream scenarios would have to be enacted only once more.

She looked around the dormitory in the slow-gathering light and saw that the other women of the family were still asleep. Myrah undid her own tether and quietly left the room. Controlling her flight by briefly touching the moisture-beaded walls with hands or feet, she made her way along a corridor to the main room. She had been hoping to get away without saying goodbye to anybody, but was gratified nevertheless to find that Lilee, the Family Mother, was waiting for her.

The old woman embraced Myrah silently before handing her a bladder of fresh water and a twist of salted white fish wrapped in edible moss. Myrah did not feel like eating, but rather than offend Lilee she bit off some of the raw fish and forced herself to chew it.

"Your mother was a strange one, too," Lilee said, watching Myrah intently.

"I don't remember her."

"You've only to look at yourself and you'll know what your mother was like." Lilee's grey hair floated lazily around her head. It had been allowed to grow long because she was too old to leave the house, and therefore never had to wear a bubble cage. Clan members who went out into the water always cropped their hair short to prevent it displacing valuable air from the cages strapped to their heads.

"Why do you say she was strange?" Myrah squeezed some water from the bladder into her mouth.

"She was always restless. Always questioning things."

"Like me, you mean."

"Yes. And she would have offered to go down, too."

Myrah tried to imagine an earlier version of herself, troubled with the same discontentment, whose life had been brought to a close by illness before any of her questions had been answered, and for a moment she was almost glad she was venturing into the darkness. It would be better to die as a result of one's own actions, in pursuit of a cause, than wait passively to fall victim to one of the casual killers, the diseases which so frequently decimated the Clan.

"I have to go now," she said.

"God go with you." Lilee came towards her, arms outstretched, and during the embrace Myrah was surprised to discover that the older woman was weeping. She felt a pang of guilt over the fact that to her Lilee was just another person, that she had done nothing to develop the bond of intimacy which existed between the other females and their House Mother. The failure on her part was all the greater because her natural mother had died so early in her life.

"They'll be waiting for me." Myrah broke free and went out into the corridor without looking back. Facing her was a structure which some Clan people called a stair—two inclined beams spanned by a series of horizontal flat surfaces—the purpose of which she had never been able to understand. She flew upwards above it, guiding herself by a rope which was passed through thin vertical posts, and emerged from the house into the blue light of the morning. Unfastening her bubble cage from her belt, she spread its petals and strapped it to her head. There was nobody to be seen in the airy vastness of the Home's central volume, something for which Myrah was glad. She kicked off from the metal rim of the Artisan house and flew upwards through a thin webwork of

53

ropes towards the Topeast entrance. Going through the clinging folds of the air net, she entered the water with full lungs
and swam the short distance to the portal in the defensive net.

Lennar and Geean were already in the sentry's bubble, and
she could see other figures in the water beyond. The scene
very much resembled the one which had greeted her at the
same place only a day earlier, but the visual similarity served
to accentuate the grim difference in the circumstances. As
soon as the trio had touched bodies in greeting, Lennar handed
Myrah a metal bubble cage of the kind used by hunters. It
was a non-collapsing type, constructed of thick copper strips,
designed to resist impacts and crushing pressures, and had
an extra strap which passed beneath the chin. Myrah strapped
it on in place of her own, tucking the latter into a storage net
to await her return.

"There's the habitat," Lennar said in a businesslike voice,
indicating a transport bag tied to the opposite side of the
sphere. "Give it a final check."

He went outside before she could reply. Myrah nodded
without resentment, aware that Lennar had shouldered a
heavy burden of responsibility when Solman had put him in
charge of the expedition. She undid the ties of the transport bag and began inspecting the air pumps and spare components within. Geean hovered nearby, looking impossibly
thin and childlike for one who was about to take part in such
a dangerous mission. Myrah was certain that Solman had
made a mistake in accepting her, even though—as soon as
his required six had gone forward—the remainder of the
Clan had felt the onus lifted from them and no others had
made the gesture of volunteering.

"I like Lennar," Geean said, obviously anxious to break
the silence.

"Is that why you're going with him?" Myrah did not
interrupt her work. "You're a fool if it is."

"Of course not." Geean sounded hurt. "Didn't Caro mean
anything to you?"

"Not much." Myrah was deliberately callous. "In any case,

getting myself killed wouldn't help her. You need a better reason than that."

"Perhaps I've got one," Geean said, and something in her voice caused Myrah to look up at her. The younger girl's face looked more immature than ever when surrounded by the metal framework of a hunter's bubble cage. Her eyes met Myrah's in timorous challenge.

"I didn't mean to be rough on you," Myrah said in softer tones. "It's just that you're so young and it seems such a...."

"I've begun to cough," Geean interrupted in a low voice.

"Oh! I...." Myrah discovered, as had happened to her many times in the past, that there was very little one could say to a friend who confesses she is dying. "I'm sorry, Geean. Perhaps it's just a flux."

"No—it hurts too much."

Myrah retied the transport bag. "Then you should stay in the Home."

"*Please*, Myrah." Geean caught her arm. "Don't tell Lennar."

"But if...."

"There hasn't been any blood. There'll be no danger for anybody."

Myrah shook her head in doubt. "But what if it starts? You could bring sharks or razorfins or hagfish in among us."

"I'll be all right for a few days, at least." Geean caught Myrah's other arm and they floated in the blue morning light, face to face, almost like lovers. "Myrah, I don't want to stay in there and just wait and wait. You can understand that, can't you?"

Myrah smiled. "I can understand that."

"Then you won't tell?"

"No."

"Thank you." Geean closed with her, awkwardly because of the bulk of the metal cages, and they clung together for a moment. Although the difference in their ages was only six years, Myrah felt as if she was comforting a small child, and her sense of the futility and unfairness of life returned in greater force than before. Instinct told her there had been a ghastly mistake somewhere—when a girl of Geean's age was grateful for the chance of a quick death—but her intellect told her that this was the inescapable human situation, and to hope for anything else was to be as naïve as those who talked about God and a life after that final rendezvous with Ka.

"We'd better go outside," she said gently.

Geean nodded, wiping her eyes, and they went out through the folds of the entrance. Lennar was waiting with the other three members of the party—Treece, the mature and strongly built woman from the Netmaker family, Harld and another young hunter named Dan who both appeared to see participation in the journey as a quick means of achieving full adult status. Harld had announced he was going for no other reason than to escape the nursery watch, but Myrah had not been deceived, and knowing the life expectancy of a hunter she did not blame him for being in a hurry to claim the sparse privileges available. Treece and Dan were two members of the Clan whom Myrah did not know well, but she guessed each was driven by a private desperation as great as her own, and perhaps even as great as Geean's.

For the purposes of what could prove to be a long excursion the group had been provided with a strong net in which to carry supplies of food and water, extra weapons and equipment, and a limited range of medicaments. Holding her breath, Myrah swam to it and put the rolled-up habitat inside. When she turned away to capture a free bubble she realised at once that the mysterious current had grown noticeably more powerful. The glimmering shoals of bubbles were migrating downwards like purposeful living creatures, and the six humans were actually having to tread water to maintain their positions with respect to the Topeast entrance.

Accustomed though she was to a zero-energy environment in which objects could usually be relied upon to remain stationary, Myrah began to get an inkling of the forces which were dragging at the Home. All the while Lennar was marshalling his little army and reminding them of necessary precautions, she stared at the haphazard slopes which curved away into the limits of visibility, for the first time seeing the Home as nothing more than a gigantic sac which might have been attached to the root columns by some unthinkable creature caring for its larvae. It dismayed her to realise that something as important as human life depended on a conglomeration of metal houses, nets and ropes retaining its precarious unity.

"That's it," Lennar said unceremoniously. "We'll go now."

A sentry who had been holding the supply net in place released it and retired back into the Topeast entrance with a wave of his arm. The bundle began to sink downwards at once and the group, taking hold of trailing ropes, formated on it. They swam slowly, scarcely exceeding the speed of the drift, to avoid adding a vector of their own to the motion induced by the current. Myrah was relieved to find that, as soon as they moved off, it was again easy to capture air bubbles. She swam automatically, mainly using her legs, her left hand gripping a rope and the other holding a tubular spear at the ready.

The six humans kept to a strict defensive pattern, facing outwards, three of them swimming upside down in relation to the others for complete surveillance of their surroundings. They knew that as they moved down into the dysphotic zone their disadvantages would increase, especially in comparison to the Horra, whose large and well-developed eyes made them admirably suited to a predatory existence in perpetual dimness.

There were other deadly enemies at those levels, particularly the eel-like hagfish and several varieties of ray, but the Horra were feared most of all because of what seemed to be a malign intelligence and the ghastly nature of their attack. A male Horra had ten tentacles, one of which also served as a penis—hunters sometimes saw them in copulation, the female's body gripped in a horrid simulation of a fist by the male's other tentacles, while the sexual arm probed into her mantle. The dread these creatures inspired in humans sprang largely from the fact that the sexual arm was also used as a weapon against them, being driven into the victim's body with lethal force.

Nobody in the Clan knew for certain if this was a standard killing technique used indiscriminately by the Horra against all vulnerable species, or if some element in the shape or scent of humans incited them to the grisly form of rape. What was only too well known was that, even when armed and trained, a human needed ice-cold nerves to survive an attack by a Horra—and that even the bravest individual could succumb to a deadly paralysis of mind and body in the actual event.

Like all other adult members of the Clan, Myrah had suffered nightmares about the Horra, and now—as she sank further into their kingdom—she fought, while maintaining the utmost vigilance, to reassure herself that none would be encountered. As the group followed the current down towards the abyssal core of the world, the light intensity gradually decreased and the colours red and green faded away completely. The swimmers saw their bodies as bluish shapes on which all features were drawn in black.

After three hours of the slow but continuous movement Myrah knew they were passing beyond the limit of any previous human exploration, and tension began to gather inside her. This was increased by the fact that the root columns, familiar backdrop to every facet of her life, began to thin out into occasional tapering tendrils. Finally they were left behind altogether, and the swimmers were descending through an unbounded universe of dark blue twilight. Although the root structures offered hiding places for enemies as well as for humans, Myrah felt dangerously exposed in the agoraphobic expanses of dim water. It disturbed her, too, to realise that the giant roots did not go on for ever and were, in fact, merely plants like all the other vegetation which grew near the surface. An alarming new thought occurred to her.

"I'm lost already," she said to Lennar. "How will we find our way back?"

"I'll take care of that." His voice, propagated clearly in the still waters, was unnaturally loud.

"I don't see how."

"Perhaps you should try to see, in case something happens to me. Have you noticed that the current has changed direction?"

"No." Myrah looked all around her, but in the absence of spatial referents found it difficult even to identify up and down. "Which way are we going?"

"We've stopped going straight down and are swinging to the east. Keep looking upwards every now and again. Learn to spot the centre of brightness and take your bearings from it."

Myrah looked in the direction he was indicating and was just about able to differentiate the upper and lower hemispheres of her surroundings. "I'm not much good at this."

"Neither am I," Treece put in from the opposite side of the group.

"All right," Lennar said. "Perhaps we'd better inflate the habitat and have something to eat. The three hunters will hold it at this level for a while and give your eyes a better chance to adapt."

While Lennar, Harld and Dan held the supply net in place against the action of the current, Myrah unshipped the habitat. She spread the curved petals of its bubble collector to form a dish and started the intake pump by blowing water out of one end of its cylinder. Holding the habitat in place in moving water had the effect of increasing the efficiency of the bubble collector and in a short time the fabric balloon was fully inflated. Myrah went into it, rounded up some trembling globes of water—bubbles in reverse—which were floating about inside and ushered them out through the entrance folds to become one with the surrounding water. She then started up the exhaust pump, satisfied herself that the pressure differential was being maintained, and signalled to the others that her task was completed. Treece came in at once with a bladder of fresh water and some food wrapped in a waterproof skin.

"It's nice in here," she said, glancing appreciatively around the dim sphere of the habitat. "Just like being inside an egg."

"Depends on whether you like the idea of being inside an egg," Myrah replied in a neutral voice.

"True." Treece unwrapped a twist of kingfish meat and tore a piece off with her teeth. "I've been watching you, Myrah —you seem very nervous."

"Nervous?" Myrah pretended to consider the word for a moment. "Perhaps it's because I don't like the idea of being eaten."

Treece chewed comfortably for a moment. "Why did you volunteer to come?"

"Somebody had to do it."

"But not you."

Myrah took the bladder of water and drank from it to give herself time to think. Until this minute she had exchanged less than a dozen words with Treece in her whole life, but the other woman appeared to have a degree of insight which she found disconcerting. Myrah began to wonder why they had had so little previous contact, especially as there was a functional link between the Artisan and Netmaker families.

"Aren't you afraid?" she said.

"I don't want to be eaten, either—but this is a chance that probably won't come up again."

Myrah felt a disturbing premonition. "A chance for what?"

"To see Ka, of course. To find out for certain."

Myrah suddenly knew why she and Treece had lived separate lives in spite of the close confines of the Home. Members of the Ka-worshipping sect were not exactly ostracised—humans faced too many common dangers to be able to afford disunity—but their dark religion created certain barriers to communication. The basic tenet was that Ka, being unimaginably huge and powerful in proportion, could have sought out and engulfed the human colony at any time—and the fact that he had chosen not to do so proved that he was benignly disposed to the people of the Clan.

Myrah was prepared to admit this as a point for discussion, although her own belief was that Ka was immobile, in some way anchored at the centre of the world, or totally indifferent to anything going on in the upper levels. But she objected to the elaborate myths, supposedly based on the account of a remote ancestor, ascribing to Ka fantastic powers which included the ability to absorb other beings, still alive, into his own body and then send them abroad as his servants. In particular, she disliked the notion that dead humans, after their gradual descent into darkness, were assimilated by Ka and partially revitalised, thus achieving a kind of afterlife. Myrah preferred to regard death as a clean and final exit from the rigours of existence.

"Why did you wait so long?" she said, concealing the unease that Treece inspired in her. "You could have swum down at any time. A lot faster than we're going now."

"I did start out once, then I realised I would never have found my way back. There'd be no point if I couldn't get back with the word."

"Perhaps Ka would have shown you the way."

Treece laughed delightedly. "I like that. You know, you're intelligent enough to be one of us."

"I'll stay as I am."

"I know—but perhaps something will happen to make you change your mind."

Myrah shook her head. "I doubt it. Besides, it looks as though we're not going down much further. The current is changing direction."

"That's because the world turns round," Treece said with calm conviction. "Currents have to flow in curves, but you'll find this one goes deep."

Myrah tried to think of a reply which would make her sound unimpressed and unconcerned, but in the pervasive dimness of the dysphotic zone it was strangely difficult to rally her spirit against the other woman's mental attack. That night, because of the way the guard rota worked out, she found herself sharing the habitat during her sleep period with Lennar and Harld. They came to her at separate times with silent advances of love, and she accepted on each occasion, glad of the reassurance that life, too, was a force beyond the comprehension of individuals.

# CHAPTER SIX

The damage to Tarrant's boat was not as bad as he had feared.

None of the bullets had passed through ribs or inter-costals, and—although the exit holes were large and ragged —they were close enough together to be cut out on one rect-angular section of skin. Tarrant reckoned he would be able to shape, key in and weld a new piece of plastic in a couple of hours, provided there were no unforeseen snags. He enlisted the help of two beachboys to unship the batteries, drag the boat high on to the sand and put it on its side.

One of the first things he noticed was that the paint had been lifted here and there in a series of small circular patches —evidence of the sucking power of the big squid which had tried to overturn him. He measured the diameter of the patches and their distance apart, and noted the figures down to give the experts something to work on later, on the assump-tion that he would be able to win their serious attention.

It was a warm, pleasant morning with a feathering of lacy cirrus across the blue dome of the sky to remind Tarrant, who still had a pilot's three-dimensional view of the weather, that eight or ten kilometres above him ice crystals were blowing in the high winds. Appreciative of the comforts of life at sea level, he took off his shirt and got down to working on the skin of his boat with a keyhole saw. He had completed two sides of the rectangular cut when he saw the portly, piratical figure of Will Somerville approaching from the direction of the jetty.

"Morning, young Hal." Somerville sat down on the palm

tree stump and used his red bandana to wipe perspiration from his forehead and neck. "Hot, isn't it?"

"It's not too bad."

"It's all right for you skinny people." Somerville ran an aggrieved eye over Tarrant's frame. "Tell me, how do you manage to stay so skinny?"

"Lean is a better word," Tarrant told him. "Lean, or hard, or fit."

"Skinny—how do you do it?"

"I work a lot and I don't eat much." Tarrant put his saw down and reached for a bottle of drinking water.

Somerville snorted loudly. "Don't give me that old story. I've seen the way you skinny guys eat and.... Say, what happened to your boat?" He stood up and came closer to inspect the damage. "It looks like somebody went to work on it with a pickaxe."

Tarrant slaked his thirst before replying. "I doubt if you'd believe me."

"Try me." Somerville's intelligent brown eyes registered concern. "Hal, is this more of the sabotage you were talking about? Because if it is...."

"No—I did this myself." Tarrant went on to describe the events at the northern rim of the farm on the previous night, presenting his story in the least sensational manner possible. He felt an indefinable relief when he saw that Somerville was listening with no sign of incredulity, even though—in the bright, commonplace surroundings of the waterfront— the words sounded strange to his own ears.

"Christ, Hal! This is serious." Somerville ran his fingers over one of the circular paintless areas on the hull. "It sounds as though you were lucky to get out of it alive."

"I was."

"Look, can I have that section of skin when you've finished cutting it out? There might be blood or some kind of residue on the inside and I'd like to get it under my microscope."

"Consider it yours." Tarrant was gratified by the other man's reaction. "I'd be interested to hear what you find."

64

"I'll bet you would. I've been going around telling everybody the sea is changing, but I didn't expect anything like this."

"Not your nitrates again!" Tarrant shook his head in amused disbelief. "Don't tell me an extra dose of salt turns an ordinary squid into a supersquid."

"No—but I'm sure there's a connection," Somerville said. He looked as though he was about to add something, but lapsed into a broody silence instead. A gull flew low overhead, disturbing the air with its wingbeats, and swung out to sea across the park-like expanses of the farm. Tarrant picked up his saw and began cutting again, using the narrowest part of the blade to effect a change in direction. He concentrated on the job for a minute, then his curiosity about what was going on in Somerville's mind became too great.

"Have you any theories about what's happening around here?" he prompted.

Somerville brightened perceptibly. "There *is* a theory which might explain most of the facts, but it's so far out and fantastic that I wouldn't bet my beer money on it."

"I promise not to laugh."

"Well...." Somerville paused for a moment, looking embarrassed. "Have you ever heard of the Bergmann Hypothesis?"

"Bergmann?" There was a stirring in the depths of Tarrant's mind. "Yes, but can you refresh my memory?"

"Right. You know, of course, that the temperature of the Earth as a whole doesn't remain constant." Somerville had launched into his exposition with a lack of hesitation which suggested he had been rehearsing his lines for a long time. "Every now and then we get an ice age, and sometimes the pendulum swings the other way and we get a freakish warm period. The Earth is coming out of a hot spot right now. It began over three hundred years ago—around the middle of the 20th century, in fact—and ever since then the polar caps have been...." Somerville stopped speaking at the sound of footsteps nearby.

Tarrant looked up and saw Kenneth Kircher approaching. His face was more solemn than usual, and Tarrant's heart sank as he guessed there was going to be trouble. After a brief exchange of greetings all round, Kircher turned his back on Somerville and stood impassively gazing out to sea, hands on hips. Somerville looked at Tarrant, wide-eyed, his jaw sagging theatrically, then made an obscene gesture in the direction of Kircher's backside.

Tarrant cleared his throat. "Did you want to talk to me, Mr Kircher?"

"Yes, Hal." Kircher did not turn around. "As a matter of fact, I did."

"What about?"

"It's quite personal, Hal."

"I have to go now," Somerville said hastily, giving Tarrant a sympathetic wink. "Don't forget to drop that section of skin off at my boat." He strode away along the beach, the ends of his crimson bandana flapping jauntily behind his neck. Tarrant indulged in a futile regret that Will Somerville, a man he could talk to, was not Beth's father.

He resisted the urge to clear his throat again. "I hope there's nothing wrong, Mr Kircher."

"What makes you think there's something wrong?" Kircher turned to face him. "Conscience, is it?"

"No." Tarrant got to his feet, still holding the pointed saw. "My conscience is clear."

Kircher sniffed. "Are you sure you know the meaning of the word?"

"Which word?" Tarrant was gripped by a heady impatience. "I think it would be better if you just told me what's on your mind."

"Very well, Hal," Kircher said. "What's on my mind is your behaviour of last night."

"I've already apologised for that."

"I'm talking about your behaviour towards my wife."

"Your wife?" Tarrant gave an incredulous laugh. "I've never shown Mrs Kircher anything but the utmost respect."

"Is it respect to keep staring at a woman, and leering at her, and deliberately showing signs of ... animal arousal?"

"Is that what she told you I did?"

"How else could I have found out? You made sure you only got up to your antics when my back was turned. Otherwise I'd have...."

"Otherwise you'd have what?" Tarrant came to an important decision about his future with or without Beth, and an irksome load was lifted from his soul. The first petty privilege associated with his new freedom was that when talking to Kircher he no longer could be blackmailed into using the formal mode of address, and he decided to take advantage of it right away. "What would you have done to me, Kenneth?"

Kircher looked slightly taken aback. "You still haven't explained yourself."

"I don't need explaining, because I'm normal." Tarrant looked into the older man's round, red-brown face, which was also illuminated from below by the glow from his orange shirt. He decided that Kircher was now as unimportant to him as the brightly coloured balloon he resembled, but his anger was far from being appeased.

"Your wife needs explaining," he continued, "because she's sick. And you need explaining, because you probably made her that way."

"Cissy was right about you," Kircher whispered. "You're a degenerate."

Tarrant put on a fixed, angelic smile and moved closer to Kircher, running his fingers along the blade of the saw. Kircher backed off, then turned and hurried away towards the jetty and the line of farm boats. Tarrant returned to his work immediately, determined to remain cool and outwardly unmoved.

He finished excising the rectangle of skin and used it as a template for cutting a replacement from a larger sheet of plastic. It took him another forty minutes to do the precise shaping, coat the exposed ribs with adhesive and spring the

67

new section into place. The most difficult part of the job completed, he connected a welding pistol to his batteries and began fusing the edges of the patch into those of the surrounding skin. As the work progressed Tarrant found his attention wandering. He had decided to remain aloof from Beth's parents, giving them no indication that he had been hurt by what they had said, and to visit her at the Export Bureau where she worked.

His hastily formed plan had been to present Beth with a straightforward choice—marry him right away regardless of her parents' views, or agree that they were to forget each other—but as the minutes went by his anger at Cissy Kircher began to dominate his thinking. It was his practice to take people as he found them, and not to fret too much when they fell short of the ideal, but there had to be a limit to tolerance at one stage or another. He reached the conclusion that Cissy had gone beyond that limit, so far beyond it that there would have to be a confrontation.

When he had finished welding Tarrant righted the shallow-draught boat, replaced the batteries and deployed the solar panels. Two hours remained until high tide. He left the craft where it was, crossed the shimmering white concrete of Front Street and walked up the hill in the direction of the Kircher residence. Kenneth Kircher was on his boat and Beth would be at work, which meant he would be able to talk to Cissy alone. As the house came into view behind its ramparts of flowering shrubs he felt a pang of anticipation coupled with a kind of nerviness which sprang from a private suspicion that, in a way, Cissy had been right about him. He hesitated at the front door for a moment, then knocked loudly. A few seconds later it was opened by Beth.

"Hal!" Her pink-flushed face showed surprise and concern. "What are you doing here?"

"I came to...." Tarrant paused, deciding against saying he had not anticipated seeing her. "What are you doing here?"

"Having a day off work. To help Mum get ready for her anniversary party."

"I see." Tarrant tried not to look at Beth's bosom, well-defined within a blouse of glistening nylon. "I'd like to speak to your mother."

"She isn't here."

"Oh." Tarrant rearranged his plans. "Aren't you going to invite me in?"

Beth gave him a roguish smile. "Do you promise not to try anything?"

"No."

"In that case—come in."

Tarrant closed the front door behind him and his heart began to pound in a slow, powerful rhythm as he saw that Beth was not retreating to one of the inner rooms. They were alone together—for the first time in their lives—in the shady privacy of the hall. He had half-expected that Cissy Kircher would by this time have succeeded in poisoning her daughter's mind against him, instead of which Beth gave the impression of being more approachable and interested than ever before. The hammering in his chest grew fiercer as it crossed his mind that hearing he was an unprincipled lecher might have served to kindle some previously dormant fire within Beth. He opened his arms to her, and she smiled her very white smile and moved closer to him. His head swimming with gratification, Tarrant savoured the moist pressure of her lips against his own.

"I love you, Beth," he whispered.

"I ... I love you, Hal." She spoke without breaking the kiss.

Tarrant strove to contain himself, to consolidate the ground he had gained before venturing any further. He was swamped by the warmth of her breasts against his chest, the movement of her thighs on his, and in between these zones of sensation a coy nuzzling which was shooting fountains of pleasure into him. He slid his hands down the firm, fluted flesh of her back, drew her more tightly against him and made one gentle, yearning thrust against her belly. Beth seemed to respond for an instant, then her body went rigid.

"What are you doing, Hal?" she said in a small, cold voice. "What do you think I am?"

"I think you're a woman," he replied automatically, his mind still submerged.

"What sort of woman?"

"How many sorts are there?" Tarrant tried to slide his hands up to her breasts, but suddenly Beth and he were apart and she was staring at him in anger.

"In spite of what you think, there *are* different kinds of girls," she said. "And I'm not the sort you're obviously used to."

Tarrant was jolted back into reality. "I'm not used to *any* sort of girl, for God's sake! I've been hanging around here for six months and this is the first time I've even got touching you."

"Is that the only thing you wanted?"

"No! It's not the only thing, but it's important." Tarrant exhaled loudly in frustration. "I want to go to bed with you, Beth. It's perfectly natural, you know—even your mother and father must have done it at least once."

"Don't talk about them like that."

"Sorry! Sorry! I shouldn't have implied that they're normal."

"You'd better go, Hal." Beth was growing pale.

"Will you marry me?"

"I said you'd better go."

"And I asked you to marry me," Tarrant shouted. "I'm not going until you say yes or no."

"I have no intention of marrying you or anybody like you," Beth said in her mother's voice.

Tarrant swore at her in desperation, incoherently, stringing together every shock word he knew, causing her to shrink back like a woman being beaten. When he had finished, knowing he had closed one door for ever, he turned and strode out of the house, jarring his heels on the ground with every step. He paused at the end of the short avenue, trying to think of some physical outlet for the fury which was surging through him. In the end he realised there was only one activity which was compatible with his mood, and he went further up the hill to fetch his rifle.

As he walked, he prayed that the big squid would come to the surface in daylight.

# CHAPTER SEVEN

In the morning they decided to keep the habitat inflated and to swim alongside it like small fish attendant on some greater creature of the sea. Lennar's reasoning was that, as well as making it more convenient to eat and rest, the bulk of the expanded habitat would discourage many life forms from coming too close. There was a lesser possibility that it might serve to attract the attention of some monstrous predator which did its feeding on a huge scale, but this was something they chose not to dwell on at any length.

Myrah knew they had travelled a considerable distance while she was asleep, because the return of day manifested itself as only a slight lessening of the general murk. Her eyes were adapting better than she had expected, however, and she had no trouble in seeing and capturing air bubbles as she swam with economical strokes, holding the habitat's outer net with one hand and keeping her spear at the ready with the other.

There was little conversation among the other members of the group and she guessed that, like herself, they were intensely aware of the vast and uninterrupted reaches of dark water through which they were moving. This was the natural element of the Horra, a creature whose large and well-developed eyes would function efficiently in the dysphotic conditions. Lennar, Harld and Dan were equipped with small cages containing shiverfish—tiny, nervous creatures who became agitated when a Horra came within range of their acute senses—but Myrah was not convinced they could give a sufficiently timely warning of danger in the present circumstances. There was, for instance, no guarantee that the band of humans were not under constant surveillance from afar by nameless and unknown entities whose vision was even more penetrating than that of the Horra.

Myrah kept her head turning constantly. Occasionally she made a sudden movement with her spear to frighten off small fish, some of them decorated with luminous spots, which came flitting in to investigate the party of strangers. This had to be done with discretion and only when a fish was particularly troublesome, because of the danger of creating an irregular pattern of movements—suggestive of a creature in difficulties —which might invite the attention of barracudas or sharks. Once she did see a shark nearby and froze into immobility, but it turned out to be a harmless variety which the people of the Clan knew as the gurry and sometimes netted for food. Its meat produced a strange intoxication when eaten fresh, which some of the young men occasionally did in spite of the danger of poisoning, but it became a useful food when allowed to dry or partly decompose.

As the elongated shape wove its sleepy way back into the gloom, Myrah noticed that Geean had turned her back to it and had pressed her face into the pliant surface of the habitat. New doubts about the girl's presence on the journey sprang into her mind and she decided to remind her of the basic rules for survival as soon as they were alone together. Although Geean's life was her own to dispose of as she wished, she had no right to endanger the others by not remaining on the alert.

The chance came some time later when Geean signalled she wanted a drink and went through the entrance fold into the habitat. Myrah indicated to Lennar that she would like to go inside as well and he nodded his permission. She found Geean clinging to the net near the intake pump, her mouth wide open as she gulped from the flow of air. The chin strap of her bubble cage was undone.

"What's wrong, Geean?" she said. "Are you in pain?"

Geean started violently at the sound of her voice, but relaxed a little when she turned and saw Myrah. "I'm trying not to cough," she said, keeping her voice low to avoid being heard by the swimmers outside. "And it hurts. It's hurting me, Myrah."

Myrah's first and instinctive thought was for her own safety. "Has there been any blood?"

"Not yet."

"Not *yet*?"

"It'll be all right," Geean whispered, coming towards Myrah. "I've brought some bags with me. Look. I won't let anything get away."

"You can't be sure of that," Myrah said accusingly. "In some places it only takes one drop to get into the water, and.... You didn't tell me you were this bad."

"I'm sorry. I'm sorry."

"That doesn't help." Myrah stared angrily into the childish, doomed face which looked so incongruous within the metal frame of a hunter's bubble cage, and suddenly her sense of the enormity of their situation returned in full force. She tried to smile, and opened her arms. Geean embraced her and they floated through the air in a slow rotation, their naked bodies clinging together in a fervour which had elements of sexuality. Myrah stroked the moisture-beaded skin of the younger woman's back and was shocked to realise just how little of her there was. It dawned on her that the very act of facing up to the daily life of the Clan with such inadequate physical resources called for a kind of courage she did not understand.

"I'm sorry, too," she said in a quiet voice.

"What's going to happen to me?"

"I'll do everything I can for you."

"I knew you would. I wish I could be like you, Myrah." Geean pulled the bubble cage off her head and kissed Myrah on the breast and navel.

"No." Myrah caught her and drew her upright. The people of the Clan had no taboos against homosexual love, and Myrah experimented with it when in certain moods, but the idea of congress with the immature and ailing girl was repugnant to her, especially as Geean had misunderstood her

74

words of reassurance. She caught the bubble cage in its slow flight towards the exhaust pump, slipped it back on to Geean's head and began fastening the chin strap.

"I promised I'd do all I could for you," she said gently. "And that means getting you back to the Home as soon as possible. I'll have to tell Lennar."

"You wouldn't! Anyway, there's nothing anybody can do now."

"We can split up the group. One of the men can take you back."

Geean caught Myrah's wrists. "I couldn't swim that far without a place to rest."

"I'm sorry, but you and Lennar will have to work that out between you." Myrah moved to free her hands, but Geean held on with surprising tenacity and a struggle developed. Losing her patience, Myrah applied her superior strength and was prising Geean's fingers open when there was a warning cry outside the habitat. The man's voice, travelling partly in water and partly in air, was unrecognisable, but Myrah had no difficulty in understanding the single, dreadful word. Geean immediately released her grip and floated back, eyes and mouth wide open. Myrah snatched their two spears from the adhesive pad near the entrance and pushed one towards Geean.

"Come on," she snapped. "Outside."

Geean shook her head. "But it's the Horra."

"We still have to go out." Myrah was turning towards the entrance when she heard the unmistakable churning sound produced by a big Horra swimming at maximum speed. An instant later the side of the habitat burst inwards and its interior was filled with a dark conical body, threshing tentacles, whorls of water, fantastically stretched air bubbles and ribbons of netting. Myrah was hurled into the netting by the impact and the rush of water through her bubble cage stripped it of air. She held her breath and fought clear of the clinging mesh.

The Horra had lost momentum with its destruction of the

habitat and it was twisting to bring its tentacles into a position in which they could encircle her. Myrah saw at once that its huge, calm eyes were out of her reach and she knew that if she was going to have any hope at all of surviving she would have to use the cold-blooded fighting technique developed by generations of the Clan's hunting family.

She identified the Horra's sexual arm by its almost total lack of suckers and grasped it with her left hand, at the same time allowing the other tentacles to snake around her body and draw her towards the beaked central mouth. At the last possible moment she brought her spear up level, instinctively positioning its blunt end in the special cup on her belt and guided the point into the Horra's mouth. The theory was that the harder the Horra tried to pull her in, the further it would drive the spear into its own stomach; but putting it into practice called for quick reflexes and strong arms. Myrah fought desperately to fend off the sexual arm and at the same time to brace the spear with her right hand.

She was dimly aware of Geean screaming nearby and of the sound of other struggles, but most of her attention was taken up with the realisation that the tubular metal of the spear was bending with every contraction of the Horra's tentacles. It had only to buckle in the middle and she was certain to die—and it seemed that this particular Horra was powerful enough to ensure that she did. She twisted the spear, hoping to force its point through the tough wall of the monster's stomach and into more sensitive regions of its body, but her efforts were having no useful effect, and a pounding in her chest told her that she had to have air very soon.

She forced her head back against one of the loathsome coils, managed to capture a bubble, and then made an even more startling discovery—the Horra was not trying to kill her.

The mind-numbing proximity of the creature made it difficult for her to think rationally, but it became apparent that the Horra was not behaving in a manner normal to its kind. It was not thrusting with its sexual arm and was no longer forcing her towards its mouth, even though its tentacles were still wrapped around her body. Belatedly, Myrah also realised that it had not used its pads to exert the fierce suction which could lift skin and flesh from a human body. It was almost as if—and she found the thought subtly more terrifying than the prospect of immediate death—the creature had set out to make her a prisoner.

Myrah moved her head again, taking more air, and for the first time had a chance to witness the complexity and confusion of the battleground. It appeared that the group had been attacked by at least twelve Horra working in unison. Two of the latter had been mortally wounded and were drifting with aimless twitches of their tentacles amid clouds of black fluid. Geean and Treece and the three men were in same plight as Myrah—each of them held fast by a Horra, in the hideous likeness of a huge fist—but all seemed to be alive and unharmed. The supply pack and the remnants of the habitat were tumbling slowly away, and as an extra bizarre touch one of the pumps had been torn free of the habitat and was swimming off into the gloom, industriously propelling itself by its exhaust, like a strange cylindrical fish. Several Horra—those without captives—were slowly circling the central group, pulsing along with regular spreading movements of their tentacles.

In spite of the evidence of her eyes, Myrah was unable to accept the idea of the Horra suddenly beginning to display human-like intelligence. They had always been dangerous adversaries, but their cunning had invariably been animalistic. For example, it had never been known for one of them to release its grip on a hunter and thereby avoid having a spear driven through its vitals. The thought led to a further notion that perhaps the Horra *had* learned to avoid that form of destruction and were trying a new battle technique of their own. Myrah strove to hold fast to her spear, then observed that Geean and Dan had lost their weapons and therefore were completely at the mercy of their captors—yet the Horra were making no move to dispatch them.

When she found she was again in need of air, Myrah's

alarm increased as she saw there were no bubbles within her reach. Suddenly she understood just how easy it would be for the Horra to kill her with scarcely any effort—it had only to prevent her from breathing for a short time. She struggled to trap a bubble in her cage and, as if to discount her latest theory, the Horra actually propelled itself into a region of plentiful air and released its coils sufficiently to permit her to take as much as she needed.

The same movement, by increasing the distance between her body and the creature's mouth, allowed the butt of her spear to come out of the belt cup, and with a convulsive twitch of one of its arms it withdrew the spear from its mouth and cast it aside. Myrah was too intent on breathing to try countering the move, but from the corners of her eyes she received the impression that the Horra holding Lennar, Harld and Treece had performed exactly the same manouevre at exactly the same time.

"Is everybody all right?" Lennar shouted. "Give me your names."

The others, with the exception of Geean, replied to him, and he spoke her name again. Myrah, who was closest to Geean, saw that she was still moving her hands and feet, and taking air in a normal manner, although her slim body was almost completely hidden by the banded alien flesh of her captor.

"She's all right," she called. "I'll watch her."

"Good for you," Treece said, with enigmatic calmness, from a nearby point in the nightmarish ballet formation.

Lennar raised his voice again, miraculously managing to regain some of his authority. "Try not to panic, and whatever you do—don't struggle. The last thing we want to do is tire ourselves out. There's something we don't understand here, but we can...."

Treece laughed sharply. "Lennar, you're a fool if you don't understand this."

"What are you saying?"

"I'm telling you these are Ka's servants." Treece gave another laugh, a curious barking sound which succeeded in adding to the horror Myrah was experiencing.

."Silence!" Lennar commanded. "We'll need clear thinking if we're going to have any...."

He broke off as the entire assembly of Horra turned in one concerted movement and began swimming downwards. There was no tentative following of a current as had been the case with the party of humans. The Horra seemed to know exactly where they were going, and they were out to get there quickly. They swam in typical Horra fashion with their pointed bodies spearing through the water followed by clusters of tentacles, from the base of which their huge, unblinking eyes seemed to regard the universe with quizzical detachment.

The rush of water through the tentacles and the hissing of their propellent siphons made it impossible for the humans to communicate with each other, but in any case Myrah would have had nothing to say. She had to concentrate all her attention on snatching air bubbles out of the turbulence created by the Horra which had her in its grip. Several times she got into difficulties as bubbles shattered and refused to glue themselves into the metal cage around her head, but always—as if sensing what was happening—the Horra swung her to one side and made it possible for her to obtain adequate air.

Try as she might, she could not avoid the conclusion that the cephalopod was behaving like an intelligent being, but for the greater part of the time she was unable to think at all. The feel of the cold, rubbery flesh against her skin, the slow working of the beaked mouth less than an arm's length away, and the oblique scrutiny of the huge eyes combined to produce in her a mental paralysis. She began to get a vague understanding of why some sea creatures yielded so readily to their natural enemies, even in some cases appearing to assist in their own destruction. Her sluggish and morbid reveries came to an end when she felt the Horra's downward rush begin to slacken.

With the drop in speed the business of staying alive required less of her attention, even though she was now taking bubbles by feel rather than sight, and she began to look around for some evidence that they had reached a destination. Below the pointed bodies of the Horra, and barely discernible in the near-lightless conditions, was a vast black solidity. Its surface was complicated and appeared to be covered with protuberances and masses of fronds which moved slowly under the action of currents. Here and there, close to the dark surface, Myrah picked out signs of independent motion which could have been more Horra or other creatures going about mysterious errands. One part of her mind, insulated from fear, began to wonder how it was possible for her to see at all in what should have been complete darkness. The answer came when she noticed that some of the moving creatures actually had glowing wakes and it dawned on her that there were quantities of luminescent material drifting in the water all around.

Here, too, was the answer to a question which had long been discussed and argued by the people of the Clan. The world did have an inner core, probably built up of the shells and skeletons of beings which had died over a period of hundreds of years. It was known from experience that the vast majority of corpses were devoured before they had sunk very far, but here was the evidence that some had reached the centre, and had been received by....

Myrah tried to fight off the concomitant thought, but it invaded her mind with irresistible power.

*This was the home of Ka!*

Somewhere down there, in cavities hewn from a grisly coral, crouched the Unknown One—the dark force which lived and yet was the antithesis of life.

Like all others of her race, Myrah had no direct evidence of Ka's reality, but she had always believed in him nonetheless. In addition to the legends which had been handed down from the ages in which humans had been able to roam the world in freedom, there was her unshakable inner certainty that Ka had to exist as a necessary complement to life as she knew it....

"Is everybody still alive?" Lennar shouted above the decreasing turbulence. There was a scattered response, in which Myrah joined without conscious volition, then she heard Harld asking a question.

"What's going to happen now?"

"We have to face up to it," Lennar replied in a strained voice. "The Horra have never wanted us for any other reason than to. . . ."

"You're a fool, Lennar," Treece cut in hysterically. "These are not ordinary Horra. These are the servants of Ka. They're taking us to Ka!"

Myrah felt a renewed awareness of the creature which was holding her in such monstrous intimacy and for a moment almost yielded to the need to scream, but Lennar's voice cut through the red mists of panic.

"Pay no attention to the mad woman," he ordered. "They aren't gripping as hard now, so this is the best time to break free. Take as much air as you can, and when I give the word—start fighting them. Go for the eyes with your feet, and if you manage to get free don't wait around for anybody else. . . ."

His voice was lost in a multiple cry, a strange sobbing gasp, which issued from the throats of the other humans. Myrah felt her own breath sighing away, adding to the chorus of despair, as the black core of the world—the entity she had taken to be an inanimate mountain of coral—spread its arms to receive them.

There followed a period of indeterminacy; of time outside of time; of fear beyond fear.

Myrah was distantly aware of spinning and tumbling as in a powerful current, of night wings curving around her and blotting out the entire universe, of a growing darkness which made it impossible for her to find air bubbles, of the bursting force within her ribs. Then there was the envelopment by Ka, the constriction of a cold and cavernous womb, the smothering pressure of its jelly-flesh on her face.

And, finally, there was her submission.

Myrah yielded with a guilty pleasure, grateful that the escape was being made so easy, and so desirable.

She drew the living tissue of Ka into her mouth and lungs.

# CHAPTER EIGHT

The tide had not fully risen when Tarrant got back to his boat, and there was nobody in the vicinity whose help he could enlist in dragging the battery-laden craft down the beach.

He stared at it for a moment, undecided, then his gaze lit on the rectangle of discarded plastic skin he had promised to give to Will Somerville. Stepping on to the tilted deck of the boat, he put the rifle and box of ammunition out of sight beside the wheel and vaulted down on to the white sand. The skin panel was warm to his touch, and when he examined its inner surface he could see brownish stains near some of the bullet holes. He looked along the line of the jetty, satisfied himself that Somerville's cruiser was at its berth, and set off walking with the panel under his arm.

A mid-morning quietness lay over the waterfront, most of the farmers being out tending their sectors, and the air itself seemed to be emitting sparkles of light. The scene affronted Tarrant with its unsympathetic cheeriness. He tried to console himself by drawing up grandiose plans for drinking sprees and—now that he was a free man again—a cold-blooded and calculating survey of the entire female population of Cawley Island which, he told himself, was bound to unearth at least one immoral and oversexed woman with whom he could form an alliance. And there was no longer anything to prevent him taking his own sea-going yacht out of mothballs and setting off to find a less restrictive society in which it would be possible to lead a normal life.

He reached the jetty and walked along the sun-dried, silver-grey planking. The lush green meadows of the algae beds spread before him to the horizon, scenting the inshore breeze. In a week or so he would be skimming off a crop for the production of high-quality protein cakes, and once that was done he would have enough gold in his pouch to support him for a year or more if he lived carefully.

*But why,* came an unsettling thought, *bother to live carefully. Why not have a three-month burn-out? There's nothing to stop you now....*

The excitement of the idea put a bounce in his step, and he found himself thanking Beth and her parents aloud as he neared Somerville's boat. They had done him a favour by making it so obvious that he could never be like them, and it was up to him to capitalise on his good fortune. Giving in to a boyish impulse, Tarrant began to whistle, hoping to impress Somerville with his jauntiness, but he found there was nobody on board the boat.

It was one of the larger craft—with a proper cabin below decks—of a type used by some of the inner sector farmers who were less concerned about transport costs. Tarrant went down into the cabin and propped his rectangle of plastic against the central table. The table was covered with glass and porcelain dishes, scraps of paper and stained cloth, pens and crayons, reference books and a cylindrical slide rule. One of the books was a good-quality atlas which lay open at oblique azimuthal projections of the northern and southern hemispheres.

Tarrant noted that somebody, presumably Somerville, had drawn a heavy blue line around the polar caps some distance out from their edges, and had cross-hatched the enclosed margin of sea. He shook his head and smiled at this fresh evidence of Will Somerville's eccentricity—full-colour atlases were hard to come by, and anybody who defaced one had to have more money than sense. Even when Tarrant had been serving with the South Newzealand Air Force he had had to make do with monochrome photocopies of air navigation charts, and would never have considered writing directly on them. He took a crayon, scribbled a note to say he would be back in the evening and left it on the atlas.

By the time he got back to his own boat there was more activity on the waterfront and he had no difficulty in enlisting aid to get himself afloat. Now that his anger had been supplanted by bright-hued anticipations of a joyously profligate future, Tarrant felt less inclined to go hunting the big squid. He considered abandoning the idea and going home to drink wine, especially as squid were known to dislike bright light; then it occurred to him that were they to return after dark and spill more of his algae crop he would be quitting Cawley Island with less money stowed away. And for the plans he had in mind he was going to need all the money he could possibly raise.

He obtained some wire with which to secure his boom connectors, and set out for the northern rim of the farm.

# CHAPTER NINE

Ka was the oldest inhabitant of his world; the first to survive the time of change.

He had begun his existence as a minute blob of protoplasm, a bud cast off into a warm ocean by a sedentary polyp. The polyp itself had been an asexual creature, little more than a vegetable in many respects, but the hydrozoan species to which it belonged could perform one of nature's most audacious tricks—the alternation of generations. Its numerous offspring had male and female characteristics, were free-swimming, and had great responsiveness to their environment. They were, in fact, medusae.

Although devoid of any kind of brain, the transparent, bell-shaped creatures—Ka among them—promptly set out to perform a lengthy and incredibly difficult task, one which would have been beyond the capabilities of any higher life form. The instinctive ambition of each medusa was to increase his size and mass by a factor of many thousands, not simply through eating and growing as is the case with most creatures, but by assimilating other medusace—alive and complete—into his own body, reducing them to the status of organs serving a greater whole.

The dangers facing the tiny organisms were great, and the probability of an individual's success very low. Many of the medusae were short-lived, a large proportion taking their unenviable place in the food chains of other creatures, some being carried by wind and current into regions where the conditions were wrong for their survival. But Ka was lucky.

In the early stages of his life he grew to a diameter of

several centimetres by capturing and eating small marine organisms, but this type of activity was insufficient to satisfy his drive for survival. Unaided, or unhampered, by any degree of intelligence, he began absorbing others of his own general kind, establishing tenuous but effective neural links which made their motor systems into extensions of his own.

Ka remained as the central bell or float of the unified colony he was building. His individual size increased, but this growth was minute compared to the enlargement of his corporate body as more and more units were added. Some of these were in their own medusa stage and were used to form swimming bells, typical of siphonophores, which moved the colony through the water. Others were polyps which performed specialised tasks such as feeling, tasting and feeding. The polyp members of the community also contributed reproductive individuals, and stinging individuals equipped with powerful nematocysts which fired barbed and poisonous threads into prey or enemies on contact.

The composite being which was Ka was now large and powerful, with tentacles hanging many metres below his multi-hued body, but as yet his history had been no different from that of any of the untold billions of hydrozoans which for aeons had lived and died in the Earth's oceans. It was not until he had survived the time of change that he entered the second and unique phase of his existence.

And the change came abruptly.

At one moment Ka was cruising—thoughtless, dreamless, mindless—on the surface of a calm, warm sea; and at the next he was at the centre of a maelstrom.

The currents which boiled and raged around him were so ferocious at this stage that sections of his body were torn away and dispersed into the surrounding water. Ka felt neither surprise nor fear. He was still without awareness of identity, merely an organic machine capable of a limited range of responses to his environment, and he reacted by contracting his body until he was carried into a zone of reduced turbulence.

As soon as the disruptive forces had abated he again began the search for food, and for other creatures to serve as replacements for the organs he had lost in the sudden turmoil. He was unperturbed by the fact that gravity no longer operated on him, that his tentacles now tended to spread uniformly in all directions instead of hanging in parallel clusters beneath the main portion of his body. He continued his primeval existence, oblivious to the more insidious and prolonged danger which now threatened him.

In the beginning the new world was small, containing only a few cubic kilometres of water, and solar and cosmic radiation sleeted through it with virtually no reduction of intensity. The bombardment of high-energy particles produced disease and death in many creatures, wrought freakish changes in the genes of others. Non-viable mutations were born and lived their truncated lives, and yet other mutations which might have been successful in a more favourable environment fell victim to the continuing assault of the universe. The hail of sub-atomic bullets found many targets in Ka's body, but his colonial structure enabled him to survive by discarding units which were destroyed or irreparably damaged.

At this stage he was still without intelligence, reacting blindly and instinctively to his environment, but the composition of his body had begun to undergo a profound change. In the conditions of zero gravity and high radiation some of his units developed unnatural complexities, and began to create their own neural pathways which linked them to similar benign mutations. As the process accelerated the original purpose of the colony was forgotten, and instead of absorbing units for a narrow range of functions it learned the principle of random usage, cannibalising higher and higher life forms for their organic components.

All the while the new world was growing in size. As the radiation levels within the globe of water dropped to an acceptable level, Ka's body slowed its rate of growth and began consolidating its gains. The nerve networks became even more complex and multi-connected, and gradually—over a period of centuries—there came awareness of identity, self-knowledge and ... intelligence.

A human being who becomes part of Ka can react in only one way, Myrah discovered. She began to scream.

Her cries did not manifest themselves physically, because there was no air to be forced from her lungs and, in any case, the relevant muscle groups were no longer under her control. She hung in the blackness, her body limp and apparently without life, but a part of her being was screaming nonetheless. Even when she began to think and take notice of her incredible new circumstances, the screaming continued —as regular as the breathing which was no longer necessary— in the lower levels of her consciousness, pulsing out its message of fear and revulsion.

From earliest infancy, like all members of the Clan, Myrah had lived in constant pursuit of air, never daring to exhale in open water without first having located a fresh bubble and made certain it was within reach. Now, taking refuge from the overall enormity of the situation, her mind began to dwell on its separate aspects, and she found herself marvelling at her ability to go on living without air. She had been told there was enough oxygen in the bloodstream to sustain life for quite a long time provided one did not panic, but this was a different phenomenon altogether. It was as if she was being nourished by a cool placenta which could take care of her bodily requirements for an indefinite period, perhaps for ever. The sensation was both loathsome and luxurious, and did not bear thinking about.

Myrah's next discovery was that, in spite of the darkness, she could see. It was not the normal clear vision she was accustomed to as a native of the euphotic zone, nor even the awareness of black upon black she had been developing near the end of the journey. Fragmentary images appeared and faded behind her eyes, like memories of dreams, sometimes superimposed on each other, sometimes reduced in size so that many could be presented at the same time. In some of them were the unmistakable shapes of the Horra. Others revealed meaningless slow movement of dark surfaces, and occasionally there were glimpses of human outlines, one of which appeared to be female.

*Am I looking at myself?* Myrah wondered, and the picture grew clearer momentarily. It was of a dead woman, with wasted limbs, and skeins of black, gelatinous threads issuing from her mouth, eyes and ears. The strands fanned away into a darkness which seemed to hide a multitude of similar horrors. *No,* Myrah pleaded, *my mother can't be here.* She fought to move her arms and legs, but nothing happened. There was only a great passivity, a sense of primeval contentment.

She suddenly found she had a perspective of centuries, a timescale against which a human lifespan was very short, and in a dim way she realised that—as a part of Ka—she was thinking Ka's thoughts, Ka's blurred, protean, multi-faceted, wordless, alien thoughts....

*First there was the Sun.*
*Then there was the Earth.*
*Then there was the sea.*
*Then there was life in the sea.*
*Then there was life outside the sea.*

*The sea is not one. In some places it is warm. In some places it is cold. At the cold cold places it ceases to be sea. It becomes white rock.*

*The Earth is not one. In some times it is warm. In some times it is cold.*

*In the cold times the white rock is more. In the warm times the white rock is less.*

*When the white rock is less the sea is more, and what is outside the sea is less. The life outside the sea did not want the sea to be more.*

*They put great shells in the sea. They were shells which make one place another place.*

*And the sea flowed into them, and then it was in another place.*

*When the Earth grew cold again the white rock began to be more and the sea began to be less. The shells turned, and the sea flowed from the second place to the first place.*

*This happened many times.*

*Then there was Ka.*

*The Earth grew warm again. The white rock began to grow less, and the sea began to grow more.*

*But the shells moved the sea from the first place to the second place.*

*Ka moved with the sea from the first place to the second place. And in the second place Ka was not one. Ka became more.*

*The Earth grows cold again, and the white rock is more.*

*The shells in the sea have turned, and the sea flows from the second place to the first place.*

*Ka is more, but Ka cannot grow less. Ka will be nothing.*

*Ka will send the Ka-Men into the shell, to the first place. The Ka-Men will break the shells, and the first place will no longer be the second place.*

*Ka will be more, and more, and more, and more. . . .*

The need to breathe again took Myrah by surprise.

There had been no possibility of escape from Ka, no refuge anywhere in the world, nor—and the knowledge was huge within her—had there been any real desire to break free. Ka and she had been one, wedded for ever, living in each other's body, thinking each other's thoughts, dreaming each other's dreams ... then she had been expelled.

Inky water pressed against Myrah's face, invading her mouth and nostrils, and she instinctively closed it out as she strove to penetrate the darkness in search of air bubbles. For an instant her eyes seemed to pick out a rectangle of blackness beyond blackness, but there was no sign of life-giving bubbles, and her body told her why. She was in the grip of a current with a strength surpassing anything in her previous experience, so fast-moving that bubbles—if they existed in it at all—would have taken the form of slim needles, impossible to capture and useless as a source of oxygen. A roaring sound filled Myrah's head and she was no longer certain whether it came from the water itself or was a sign that she was drowning. Her ribcage heaved convulsively as the involuntary muscles, locked in battle with her will, demanded that she breathe anything at all, even if it was the water which would bring lasting peace. Myrah spun this way and that, her arms and legs moving helplessly in the swirling violence, and the turbulent thundering of the water increased to an unbearable pitch.

Suddenly, impossibly, she was swimming in warm, sunlit water.

Myrah's first disbelieving glance took in a universe of bright water which was green rather than blue, a fleeting vision of other human shapes, and quantities of silvery bubbles swarming upwards around her. She tried to capture a bubble, but it flew vertically away from her, glinting and shivering like a living creature which was rushing towards an urgent destiny.

At the same moment she became aware of a curious sensation in her ears, an internal movement which caused an odd wrenching of her perceptions, but everything was secondary to the crushing need for air. She struck out in pursuit of the bubbles and found herself travelling upwards with unexpected speed, as though impelled by an invisible hand. The bubbles kept eluding her, and her desperation increased as the pressure within her lungs grew irresistible. An undulating blanket of silver and blue appeared just above her and Myrah sobbed in panic as she saw she was, without being able to do anything to prevent it, on the point of bursting through the surface of the world....

Blinding brilliance. Warmth. *Air!*

Myrah threshed on the surface, anticipation of the silent death negating her normal responses; then came the realisation that she was breathing dry and pure air, and that all she had to do to go on breathing it, without effort, was to lie on her back. She forced herself to relax, capacity for surprise all spent, and concentrated on flooding her system with the bounteous oxygen. The air she was taking in had a freshness far beyond anything she had ever known. It was warm, dry, scented with unknown perfumes, and as she continued to draw it into her body there came a strange new idea, timid and tentative at first, but rapidly blossoming into conviction.

*This*, she thought in wonderment, *is a place for living!*

She partially opened her eyes, but immediately had to squeeze them shut again because of the pain caused by the sun. The after-image it left was a perfect circle, which meant the Clan elders had been right in one of their stories. The sun actually was a ball of light, but she had looked at it without coming to any harm—and according to Clan teaching she should have died the silent death on passing through the surface of the world.

*But this isn't the world.* Half-memories began to stir. *This is the place called Earth.*

Myrah raised a hand to shield her eyes from the sun and made yet another discovery—a powerful, insistent force was trying to push her arm back down into the water. She used all her strength to keep it aloft, and in its shadow she managed to part her eyelids a short way and keep them open. Droplets of water were detaching themselves from her hand and forearm, and were falling back into the sea with bewildering speed. Intrigued by the phenomenon, Myrah wriggled her fingers and caused a few more drops to rain on her face, then her arm grew tired and she let it splash down on to the water. The sound reached her ears with peculiar clarity and was followed by a similar noise a short distance away.

She rolled over, marvelling at the way in which the surface of the water remained flat and intact all around her instead of breaking up into drifting globes. In her new position the sun's rays were not spearing straight into her eyes, and she was able to see more of her surroundings. The sea was a vivid blue-green which spread away beneath a canopy of featureless blue immensities. Myrah had no previous experience with vision on such a scale, and she would have plunged her face down into the water to escape the mental pressures had she not seen Lennar close at hand.

"Myrah? Myrah!" He swam closer to her. "Are you all right?"

"I think so." Myrah's neck grew tired and she had to lower her head briefly before speaking again. "But I can't hold my head up."

"Take off your bubble cage."

"What good will that do?" She looked at Lennar again and saw that he had removed his own cage. The marks left by the retaining straps glowed intensely pink against the whiteness of his skin. Myrah unstrapped the copper cage from her head and was amazed at the way in which it dragged her arm downwards, painfully twisting her fingers. She let go and the thick metal artifact plummeted into the depths. Myrah, who had intended the cage to float beside her, grabbed for it, but it had already vanished from sight.

"Let it go," Lennar advised. "I don't think you'll ever need it again."

"But...." Myrah began to feel afraid of the huge, bright, unfamiliar world all around her. "What happened to it?"

"It fell. Or it sank. The same thing happened in the Home when you let something go. It took a lot longer, that's all."

The explanation, far from reassuring Myrah, made her feel more threatened than ever. She sensed that Lennar had just told her something monstrous about their strange new environment. She had already seen how incomprehensibly large it was—but what if falling or sinking speeds were proportionate to size? What if ...?

"Help me with Geean," Lennar said firmly.

Myrah drew back from the conceptual abyss and looked around her. Without the drag of the bubble cage she was able to raise her head higher, and this time—in spite of the

94

punishing brilliance—she saw other figures spread out on the surface. The two-dimensional arrangement of forms which was imposed by the conditions made identification difficult, but she recognised Harld and Treece who were treading water on either side of Geean. Their faces seemed longer, the muscles subtly altered. Geean's hair was a striking coppery red in the direct sunlight, and it came to Myrah that they had entered a universe in which the perception of colour was a much richer experience than she could have imagined.

Harld was trying to unstrap Geean's bubble cage and keep her head above water at the same time. The girl's eyes were closed, but the controlled movements of her limbs showed that she was alive. Myrah swam to her and helped remove the heavy cage which, as with her own, sped into the depths as soon as she released it. Something about the finality of its descent triggered an alarm in her mind.

"Where is Dan?" she said.

"I think we've lost him." Lennar's face was strangely impassive. "There's nothing we can do about it."

"Shouldn't we go down and look for him?"

"How? There's no air down there?"

"I'd forgotten." Dan's death was a trivial matter, Myrah suddenly realised, only significant in that it reduced their number from six to five. "The shells are far from here," she heard herself saying. "How will we reach them?"

"Earth is the home of the human race," Lennar replied. "The humans here can travel through the water at great speed. They will help us."

"Supposing they don't want to help?"

"Ka will see that they do," Treece put in, smiling. "Nobody can refuse Ka anything."

"But Ka isn't here."

"Isn't he?" Treece met Myrah's gaze squarely, and her smile grew wider. Salt water splashed over her face and into her mouth, but she appeared not to notice.

Myrah was suddenly afraid of Treece and turned away from

her, but there was no escaping the alien presence behind her own brow. She understood then that she was still wedded to Ka, and that he could claim her at any time. The knowledge should have been insupportable—and the fact that she could accept it showed that she was no longer her own self....

"We may not be able to find anybody," she said, trying to avoid the downward spiral of her thoughts. "The Earth is so big."

"But the humans here are many. Look!" Lennar raised himself higher in the water and pointed at something in the distance.

Myrah forced her head upwards against the unceasing pull of the planet and looked in the direction Lennar had indicated. The abundance of light reflecting from the sea created a painful shimmering across her vision, but she picked out a low shape which was moving silently through the brilliance. The object was about the size of a large shark, and—using knowledge which was not her own—Myrah identified it as a boat.

By narrowing her eyes to slits she was able to discern that the boat had a single occupant.

She sank down into the water again and—silently, with their arms moving in unison—the group swam towards the lone sailor.

# CHAPTER TEN

During the ride out to the northern rim of the farm Tarrant had used an ultra-fine saw to split the bullets in six cartridges. This had rendered them useless for anything but close-range shooting, but he had the comforting knowledge that he was now equipped to punch fist-sized holes through any sea creature, no matter how large, which came near his boat.

Reaching the end of the channel, he made a tight turn to the east and cut his motor. He looked along the slowly undulating line of the boom and, as he had expected, there was no sign of intruders or anything else out of the ordinary. One of the first things he had learned about hunting, whether for game or enemy aircraft, was that no quarry was ever obliging enough to show up exactly where anticipated. He nuzzled the boat to a halt at the first set of boom connectors and tied a length of wire around the plastic pins.

The warm green smell from the hectares of protein-rich soup was overpowering as he began a slow advance to the next joint, and by the time he had reached the fifth he was heartily sick of the whole project. In his impatience he approached the joint at too great a speed and had to brake by leaning over the side and grasping a connector loop. The boat swung wilfully around its prow and he found himself at full stretch just above the water, clinging to the slick plastic with his hands while trying to draw the boat back under him with his knees.

He was so intent on the struggle that it was several seconds before he became aware of the round, plate-sized object shimmering under the surface of the water just below his face. He stared down at it for a moment, bemused, then it moved slightly, and there was movement all about it, and he realised he was looking into the eye of a big squid.

Tarrant was unable to suppress a moan of panic. He contracted his body violently, trying to snap shut the menacing space between the boat and the boom, but it closed with agonising slowness, and all the time the great, rueful eye gazed up at him from a distance of less than an arm's length. As he was on the point of recovering his balance the eye abruptly disappeared, the water heaved and he tensed for the encircling slap of a tentacle. The dreaded contact did not take place and in another instant he had thrown himself backwards into the boat.

He scrambled to his feet, picking up the rifle at the same time, and lunged to the opposite gunwale. Three of the monstrous and now-familiar shapes were spearing away to the north, the fluttering of their lateral fins churning the clear water. One of the squid was larger than the others and Tarrant recognised its mottled colouration. He threw the rifle to his shoulder for a quick shot, then froze with his finger curled around the trigger as he saw what had lured the squid away from him.

There were five people in the water less than a hundred metres from his boat.

Tarrant gaped at the swimmers in dawning appreciation of their danger. Appalled and baffled, he turned to the boat's controls, selected maximum speed and swung north in pursuit of the squid. The little craft surged forward responsively, but the tentacled shapes were lost to sight beneath a welter of reflections and he had no way of knowing how far they were ahead of him.

"Look out!" Tarrant had a feeling his voice was being carried away in the sea breeze. "Look out below you!"

The swimmers came on steadily and he saw that three of them were women. Suddenly one of the men went beneath the surface and reappeared a second later in the grasp of a dark brown squid. A woman screamed as the water around the others began to boil with submarine activity.

Tarrant shut down his motor and skidded the boat into the edge of the group, colliding with the squid which had taken the man just as it was turning over to dive. The monster was visible alongside for perhaps a second, but Tarrant's aerial gunnery training made the shot an easy one. Holding the rifle in one hand, he blasted a hole through the conical forebody. There was an explosion of inky fluid, followed by a raucous bark, and the squid released its victim.

Holding the boat in the tight circle, Tarrant sought another target. He glimpsed a massive, complex form slipping away beneath his stern and pumped two shots at it, sending foamy white trails far down into the water. The squid vanished from his view and all at once the sea was calm again, except for the sporadic movements of the man who had almost been lost. His unnaturally white skin was marked by a number of circular red blotches.

"Get him up here." Tarrant pointed at the injured man and gestured for the others to lift him on board. They swam to aid their companion and Tarrant was jolted to see they were naked except for narrow belts at their waists. He caught hold of the man's arm and dragged him over the gunwale, noticing as he did so that although the stranger appeared to be well nourished he was extremely weak. His lack of strength suggested he had been in the water a long time, yet he bore no traces of sunburn or exposure. While Tarrant was laying him out on the deck he stared about him in silence, through slitted eyes, seemingly fascinated by everything he saw.

"Next," Tarrant said to the group in the water, and a slim red-haired girl was offered up to him.

She was even weaker than the man had been, apparently semi-conscious, and was unable to assist herself into the boat. Tarrant had to lift her in his arms and a pounding awareness of her nudity surged through him. It was accompanied by a feeling of guilt over taking advantage of her distress, but as he was putting her down beside the man he could not help examining her body in the bright sunlight, fascinated by all the ways in which femininity asserted itself in the topography and proportions of the human frame.

He felt the boat rock slightly and turned to see that another girl had managed to draw herself up on the gunwale and was looking at him. She was a brunette in her early twenties, with an oval face which might have been beautiful except for its extreme pallor and a squeezed look about the eyes which suggested her sight was very poor. She gave him a direct, knowing smile which disturbed his pulse.

"Help me," she said, moving her shoulders in a way which made it clear that she was a perfectly developed woman. Tarrant went to her and assisted her into the boat. A part of his mind was puzzled by the way in which her obvious physical well-being contrasted with the lack of strength which made it impossible for her to stand up unsupported. She leaned heavily on him as he helped her lie down beside her companions, and—incredible though the idea seemed— he was almost certain she was unconcerned about the necessary bodily contacts. As soon as she was stretched out on the deck beside the red-haired girl she screened her eyes from the sun and smiled at him again. Tarrant felt a dryness develop in his mouth.

He turned away quickly and helped the remaining swimmers aboard. They were a prematurely greying woman in her thirties, and a fair-haired boy in his late teens. As with the others, they gave every appearance of fitness, yet virtually collapsed on the deck and lay breathing deeply like athletes at the end of a strenuous race. Tarrant picked up his rifle and scanned the waters on each side of the boat, satisfying himself that the big squid had been driven off. He turned back to the rescued swimmers and, now that the sense of urgency and danger had been removed from the situation, suddenly became aware of how closely the scene before him resembled his orgiastic imaginings.

"What happened?" he said, anxious to talk. "Was there a shipwreck?"

"We come from the second place," the injured man said, frowning with pain, and Tarrant belatedly remembered he had a medical kit. While he was fetching it from its cabinet, he was struck by the fact that although the stranger had spoken fluently his pronunciation had been unusual. Curiously, it reminded him of archaic speech from 20th century films and radio recordings.

"What's your name?" Tarrant opened the white-painted box and took out a container of antibiotic powder.

"Lennar."

"Where is this second place you come from?"

The man rolled his head sideways and glanced at his companions. "It is another place. Not on Earth."

"I don't get you." Tarrant began to wonder if he was dealing with a case of delirium. "How long have you been in the water?"

"We have always been in the water."

"Sorry?"

Lennar breathed deeply before speaking the strangely accented words. "The second place is made of water. It is all water."

"You'd better get some rest," Tarrant said quietly. "I'll patch you up now and get you ashore as soon as I can." He moved to begin dusting the oozing circular wounds, but the man drew back in obvious alarm.

Tarrant showed him the plastic container. "It's just a general purpose antibiotic."

Lennar stared into Tarrant's face for a moment, coming to a decision, then he relaxed and allowed himself to be treated. Tarrant took some cotton and had begun cleaning the wounds which ran in a diagonal line across Lennar's chest when he noticed the circular patches of old scar tissue on his shoulders and arms. He stopped work for a moment, wondering, and touched the scars.

"What did this?"

Lennar's lips quirked. "The Horra and I are old enemies."

"Is that what you call the big squid? The Horra?"

"That is their name."

"I didn't know they had a name." The pressure on Tarrant's

subconscious became greater. "Nobody around here had even seen one until yesterday."

"The new current has brought them here from our world."

Tarrant started dusting the fresh wounds. "And your world is made of nothing but water?"

"That is correct."

"Then how did you breathe?"

"There is some air there, but the air and the water do not remain separate. The big bubbles move slowly and we capture them in cages strapped to our heads."

Tarrant looked closely at Lennar and saw horizontal indentations such as might have been made by straps running across his forehead. He turned to the rest of the group, pleased at having an excuse to gorge his eyes on the women, and was able to pick out similar markings on their foreheads. In addition, the fair-haired youth had several old, circular scars on his chest and thighs. The brunette smiled again as Tarrant's eyes met hers, and it was apparent that she was not discomfited in any way at having her nakedness on display before him. Astounded at his own brazenness, he allowed his gaze to travel down her body and back to her face. Her smile grew warmer. Tarrant swallowed and looked away, trying to recollect his thoughts.

*The Bergmann Hypothesis!*

That was what Will Somerville had begun to outline for him only a few hours earlier, but at the time Tarrant had been able to recall little more than the name. Now, his memory goaded by new knowledge, he could assemble fragments of the fantastic theory. The Earth's overall temperature had risen sharply by the end of the 20th century, and eventually this had led to a major reduction in the size of the polar caps. It had been calculated that the water set free should have caused the sea level to rise far enough to inundate vast tracts of land. In the event, the polar caps had shrunk as predicted, but there had been no significant rise in the level of the sea, and the land areas had remained as they were.

Had this occurred during the crest decades of the 20th

century it would have resulted in scientific detective work on an unprecedented scale, but a hundred years later the peoples of the Earth had more pressing problems on their minds. Nature was restoring her balances by means of careless and casual genocides, and few people had time to concern themselves about a non-event such as the ancient coastlines enduring as they had always done.

Ulrich Bergmann had been an exception. He was a Scandinavian geophysicist who had achieved short-lived and dubious fame by asserting that in prehistoric times there had been a superior technological civilisation—indigenous to Earth, or an interstellar colony—which had taken measures to stabilise the sea level. His theory was that, positioned in perhaps a dozen places around the globe, there were huge underwater regulators. These were "matter transmitters", fitted with sensors and automatic controls, which came into operation when the Earth entered a warm period.

The excess water released from the polar caps was instantaneously transported to a suitable storage point in another part of the Solar System, where it formed a planetoid around an orbiting matter transceiver. At the end of a hot spot, when the caps were beginning to expand and lock up water, the whole system went into reverse, thus maintaining the planetary equilibrium....

Tarrant now had to decide whether or not he could accept the Bergmann Hypothesis and some of its possible corollaries.

He kept his head down, his hands busy with the work of cleansing wounds and taping pads over them, while he tried to marshal and evaluate the evidence. Will Somerville had told him that the Earth as a whole was cooling down, and that the "sea was changing". Those facts agreed perfectly with the Hypothesis; and from there it was only necessary to assume that the ocean's regulators, the sunken matter transmitters, were devices which could transport living matter without harming it. He could presume they were intended to remain on the bed of the sea and draw off nothing but water— but even the super-machines of a super-race could eventually malfunction, become erratic in their mode of operation.

He had no idea of how a matter transmitter might work, but he could visualise an intangible "entrance", a region of space which was somehow given congruency with a distant location between the planets. If the entrance became subject to fluctuations in size or position it might swallow submarines, ships or even aircraft, together with volumes of air. Tarrant's mind baulked at imagining the trauma and subsequent hardships the crews would have had to endure in order to survive in their new environment. The death rate would have been appallingly high, close on a hundred per cent, but human beings could be fantastically adaptable provided they were given the smallest toehold. As long as there was food—available in the form of fish—and ... Tarrant frowned as a new thought occurred to him.

"Is your world made of salt water?" he said to Lennar, who was watching him closely.

Lennar nodded. "It is the same water as in your sea."

"Then what did you drink?"

"We collected ice from the surface and melted it inside bags of skin."

"What good would that do? Frozen sea water is just as salty as unfrozen sea water."

"On Earth—maybe." Lennar had begun to sound tired. "But on my world the sun changes the surface water to mist during the day. At night the mist becomes water again and then turns to ice. We gather the ice near dawn, and it makes good water for drinking."

Tarrant nodded, suddenly convinced that all he had been told was true. If Bergmann's watery planetoid was rotating its inhabitants would experience day and night. Water would evaporate to form a cloud layer on the sunward hemisphere, and when the vapour was carried around to the night side it would condense and freeze. The ice would indeed yield drinkable water, but the difficulty with which it would be obtained was indicative of the general hardships of life in the artificially created world. It dawned on Tarrant that the people he had taken from the sea had just come through one of the most shattering experiences imaginable, and he began to feel a deep respect for their fortitude.

"Would you like some fresh water to drink now?" Tarrant looked along the row of faces and felt a feathery breath of uncanniness when all five, including the semi-conscious red-head, nodded once in perfect unison. His thoughts on the matter remained half-formed under the continuing visual impact of three female bodies reflecting the sunlight like miniature snowcapes. He was in the grip of what Kircher had referred to as animal arousal and could not disguise the fact, but he had a distinct impression that such things were unimportant, or unremarkable, among the unearthly men and women. Fetching a jerrycan of spring water from the cockpit, he gave Lennar a drink from a plastic cup, supporting his head as he did so. Lennar took a cautious sip, then eagerly drained the cup.

"It's good," he whispered. "I didn't know water could be so good. There was always a little salt."

"Have some more."

Lennar shook his head. "Give some to Geean."

Tarrant moved to the red-haired girl, lifted her up a little and let her drink. Her back and shoulders felt too frail, and he detected a rasping vibration each time she breathed. He raised his eyes to Lennar, who nodded significantly.

"This girl needs medical attention," Tarrant said. "I'd better get her ashore as soon as possible."

He refilled the cup and turned to the brunette, who raised her shoulders unaided to allow him to slip his arm underneath. The movement, identical to a preliminary for love, sent hot gusts of unreason billowing into Tarrant's head. While she was drinking, the girl moved closer to him and—apparently to improve her balance—placed one hand squarely on his crotch and allowed it to remain there. Tarrant almost gasped aloud with the pleasurable shock. He held perfectly still, afraid to move, until she had finished the water.

"Thank you." Her lips were glistening wet as she looked up

at him. Suddenly he was certain he was being invited to kiss her, and that, furthermore, none of her companions would consider his action the least bit out of the ordinary. *This has to be one of those dreams*, he thought. He began lowering his face to hers, acting out his part in the erotic fantasy, then became aware that the others were watching intently. Shame flooded through him on the instant, and he drew away from the girl. The look of disappointment on her face was unmistakable, and it haunted him all the while he was giving water to the older woman and the youth.

"Look," he said finally, "this has all happened too fast for me. I guess I'd better take you to the island."

Lennar looked alarmed. "We're not ready. It's too much...."

"Then we've got to have a talk and decide what we're going to do."

"We'll tell you as much as we can," Lennar replied in his strange, flat-vowelled English, "but can we cover our eyes? The light hurts."

"I'll see what I've got." Tarrant thought for a moment, then opened his equipment locker and produced a wide roll of black insulation tape, from which he tore off five pieces and improvised eye shades. While he was working another boat emerged from the mouth of the channel, a hundred or so metres away. Its owner exchanged salutes with Tarrant before swinging round to the west, heading for his own sector. Tarrant was glad the man had not pulled alongside him for a chat—he would not have relished trying to explain the presence of nude men and women in his boat. He could foresee all kinds of problems when he brought them ashore to encounter the staid and conservative populace of Cawley Island. To forestall visits from other farmers, he started his electric motor and headed due north at low speed. While the boat was cruising he learned as much as he could about his passengers.

The exchange of information was hampered by language difficulties and basic incompatibilities in outlook. Some of the words in Lennar's restricted vocabulary had no meaning at all for him, and others proved to be debased Spanish and French, but he slowly gained a general idea of what life must have been like in a space-borne globe of sea water. His sense of wonder increased as he heard that there were almost two hundred men, women and children living in a conglomeration of nets and the hulls of old ships ... that they had lost all knowledge of their origins ... that they lived far below the surface to avoid extremes of temperature ... that respiratory diseases were endemic and kept life expectancy to about thirty years....

In return, Tarrant tried to impart information which would help the group adjust to the change in their environment, but he was handicapped in that so many essential cornerstones of knowledge were missing. They had, for example, no conception of astronomy, and this made it virtually impossible for him to explain anything about the distances they had covered, apparently instantaneously, or about the size of the Earth as compared to the world they had known. Also, the rudimentary edifice of their physics—born of conditions in which gravity was almost non-existent—had little room for the concept of weight, the suddenly-acquired property which made it so difficult for them to move when not buoyed up by water.

During the halting discussions the red-haired girl, Geean, gradually came out of her state of shock and soon afterwards complained of skin pains. It took Tarrant only a few seconds to diagnose incipient sunburn, and he cursed himself for not having realised that skin which had never known direct sunlight would be highly sensitive to ultraviolet radiation. He unfurled the boat's canopy and stretched it taut between the four uprights of the solar panel array, creating a prism of shade.

"I should have thought of that sooner," he said ruefully, and was on the point of sitting down again when he noticed a boat overtaking him from the south. There was no question but that the boat was purposefully aiming for a rendezvous. Tarrant stared at it, both surprised and resentful, then he recognised the broad beam and chipped blue paintwork of Will Somerville's cruiser, *The Rose of York*. His resentment promptly faded—there was no man he would rather have had join him at that particular time—but he was at a loss to know why Somerville should have chosen to sail out this far in search of his company.

"Why haven't you got a radio in that peanut shell?" Somerville shouted from his upper deck as he reduced speed and brought his boat wallowing close to Tarrant's.

"What's the matter?" Tarrant asked.

"Who said anything was the matter?" Somerville threw his wheel over and touched fenders. "I've got something to show you, that's all. I put a few scrapings of your squid blood under the microscope, and damn me if...." His voice dwindled into silence as, from his superior elevation, he glanced down at Tarrant's deck.

"You'd better come aboard," Tarrant told him. "I've got something to show you."

Two hours later Tarrant and Somerville, by mutual consent, retired to the cabin of *The Rose of York* where they could talk without distraction. The cluttered, homely surroundings brought Tarrant some relief from the fierce psychic pressure, composed of strangeness and blatant sexuality, which was being exerted on him by the five interplanetary castaways. Even so, visions of Myrah's full-breasted nakedness and quick, bold smile were so clear in his mind that they seemed to be superimposed on everything he looked at. He was grateful when Somerville opened a locker and took out a bottle of dark rum and two glasses.

"We're in a funny situation here," Somerville said, pouring generous measures. "In the old days this would have been an international matter, and the League of Nations or the United Nations or some outfit like that would have taken it out of our hands. Nowadays, on Cawley Island, there's only you and me."

Tarrant inhaled the rich caramel aroma of his drink. "You don't have to get involved, Will."

"Are you kidding?" Somerville looked indignant. "I'm in it up to here, young Hal—don't forget I knew there was something weird going on long before anybody else did. You couldn't prise me out of this one with a crowbar."

"Okay, but what do you suggest we do?"

"It's obvious they have to be taken ashore as soon as possible. Then there'll be the job of convincing the Chamber our new friends are what they say they are and not shipwreck survivors. Kircher's in the Chamber this year, isn't he?"

Tarrant nodded gloomily. "He'll probably think I'm importing staff for a brothel."

"Well, that's a practical point to be dealt with right off— we have to get them some clothes. They'll need protection from the sun, anyway." Somerville swallowed his rum and sat staring at Tarrant with an expression of jocular dismay. "Do you feel as if the top of your head's going to blow off?"

"I'm having trouble taking it all in." Tarrant sipped his own drink. "Funny thing is, they don't seem particularly shocked or worked up. Did you notice?"

"They probably don't realise what has happened."

"They know enough. Christ, Will, they were out hunting fish, then a current pulled them into a black hole, and a second later they were in a world where everything, *everything*, is different from everything they have ever known. I mean, they're entitled to be having hysterics...."

"Delayed reaction?"

"No reaction, more like. And there's the busty one—Myrah —I swear to God she's ready for a tumble."

"Wishful thinking."

"No. It's true."

"Are you complaining?" Somerville topped up the glasses. "We established they have a low birth rate and a high death rate—so they have a different outlook on sex."

"I know, but...." Tarrant shrugged helplessly. "You and your bloody Bergmann Hypothesis!"

"Don't blame me, old son," Somerville said. "You have to admire Bergmann, though. Everything was against him, and yet he was in there first. You know he tried to institute a sky search to find his planetoid?"

"No luck?"

"Nobody was interested, as far as I know. Then he tried looking for the actual machines. There was a place off Japan where a lot of ships had been disappearing, and I think there was another one near Bermuda, and he reckoned that if he could...."

"Will!" Tarrant rattled his glass on the table. "What am I going to do with those people out there in my boat?"

A look of resignation spread over Somerville's face and he gathered up his bottle and glasses. "We'd better transfer them in here. Then we can go back to the island and still be able to keep them out of sight till we find some spare clothes."

"Let's get on with it, then." Tarrant went up on deck ahead of a grumbling Somerville, and climbed down into his own boat. Five faces turned towards him.

"We're going to take you on to Will's boat, where there's a lot more room," he said quietly. "Then we'll see about some food."

Lennar was at the starboard side, nearest *The Rose of York*. Tarrant began with him and was relieved to note that he was not actually helpless, being able to raise himself with minimal assistance to where Somerville could grasp his arms. Geean was next, and while he was stooping to lift her slim body Tarrant saw that Myrah was watching him from beneath her eye shade with what seemed like wicked amusement. He smiled at her, wondering if she understood what she was doing to him, and felt a pang of disappointment as he realised that had she been at the end of the row, nearest the port side, they would have had the chance to be alone for a minute when he had taken the others off. He carried Geean to Somerville's waiting arms, and discovered that she too, although coughing silently, was regaining some measure of strength and was able to support some of her own weight.

"Good work, young lady," Somerville said to her and raised his eyes to Tarrant. "I've just remembered I've got some Streptosyn capsules in the medicine chest. I'll get them out and start feeding them to her."

Geean looked from one to the other with concern. "It's all right," Tarrant told her. "We're going to cure that cough of yours."

She nodded gravely, and once more Tarrant was surprised by a lack of response. He had gathered enough during his earlier talks to know that Geean's people regarded bronchitis as a fatal illness, and he failed to see how she could take the news of her reprieve so calmly. It occurred to him that he might not be making enough allowance for the dissimilarity in their backgrounds, that the word "cure" might have no meaning for Geean. He turned back to the others and found that the youth, Harld, was actually rising to his feet.

"Take it easy," Tarrant cautioned, gripping the outstretched arms. "You're still new around here."

"I'm a hunter," Harld said, grinning. "I have to be strong."

"Just don't overdo it." Tarrant helped him step over the remaining two women and got him into Somerville's boat, and when he turned round he saw Myrah helping Treece to her knees. He caught Treece's circling hand and brought her across the boat. Somerville had not reappeared, and he had to stand waiting with his arms around Treece. She leaned against him more than seemed necessary, making his body hypersensitive to wave-like changes of warm pressure as she altered her posture. *It's dream time again,* he thought, as it became obvious there could be nothing accidental about what she was doing. He began to wonder, as the fevers rose into his brain, if all the women in that distant globe of water could be raging nymphomaniacs. The supposition was anything but logical, and yet....

"Hand her over," Somerville said, appearing above him. "I'm doing all the work and you're having all the fun."

Tarrant helped Treece into the bigger boat and turned back for Myrah. She was sitting nearly upright, with arms splayed behind her, but when he got close she sank back on the deck. Kneeling beside her, he faced the prospect of sliding his hands under her body to raise her up, knowing that if he did so his self-control was going to fail. He hesitated, his mind a dizzy pendulum.

"Hal," she whispered, "please swim with me."

"I.... The water isn't safe," he said, taking refuge in obtuseness, but unable to prevent his body sinking down closer to hers.

She wriggled her shoulders impatiently and the movement was transmitted to her breasts. "That isn't what I mean."

"I know." Feeling that the seconds of privacy were going fast, that he had to seize the chance while he had it, Tarrant pressed his mouth to hers. She remained perfectly still for a moment, so rigid that he began to fear a Beth-type rejection, then her lips slowly parted, inviting that first symbolic act of penetration. He probed urgently and ecstatically with his tongue, and felt something cool and liver-smooth dart forward into his mouth. It vibrated in the back of his throat. He rolled away from Myrah, retching in a frantic effort to expel the invader, but his throat was clear again and he knew that the eel-like thing—predator or parasite—was deep inside him.

He lurched to his feet, unable to speak, pointing accusingly at Myrah—then a vast, cold sadness descended over him. He knew how dark it was at the centre of the world. He felt the new current intensify its grip on his body, threatening to end his life by wrenching his component organs apart and dispersing them into the night....

"We'd better hurry," he said to Myrah. "We haven't got much time."

# CHAPTER ELEVEN

As a child of Ka, Tarrant was in exactly the same position as Myrah or Lennar—he had become one unit in a composite identity. Like a cell in the body of a human being, he retained all the autonomy that was necessary for him to continue functioning in an efficient manner, but his activities were subordinate to the needs of the gestalt being that was Ka.

At the same time, because the medusa principle is one of reciprocal benefit, his relationship with the overlord was special in that he had a unique contribution to make to the store of knowledge. Not only was his mind the best stocked of any that had ever become available to Ka, but it provided the longest baseline, the philosophical perspective and parallax without which a pool of data can never be effectively organised. Until then Ka had been limited to what he could harvest from the rare human who had strayed into the deep territory controlled by the Ka-Horra—Treece had been one such—but their world-view had been pitifully limited. He had usually returned them to the Home as free-swimming extensions of his own neural system, which had enabled him to monitor the activities of the humans from afar.

To Ka the human colony had represented an important reserve of mobility and intelligence, and he had nurtured it for centuries, sometimes sending armies of the Ka-Horra out to do battle with the Horra when it seemed that the latter were about to engulf the humans. On these occasions some of the Ka-controlled squid had perished, which meant that in a small way Ka himself had died for the sake of the humans, but his instincts had told him the sacrifices would be worth while. And, finally, he had been proved right....

Had there been time for him to be introspective, Tarrant might have found elements of his old personality cowering in an obscure, safe cranny of the mind-brain matrix. That helpless, reduced version of his former self would have been numb with dismay at the thought of a sliver of Ka's mutated nervenet curling in his right lung, but to Ka-Tarrant its presence within his body was both natural and welcome. The only matter worthy of his attention, the only thing of importance in the entire universe, was the desperate need to find the Bergmann machines and destroy them before it was too late.

He raised Myrah to her feet and helped her to the side of the boat. Somerville had not yet emerged from the cabin so he left Myrah sitting on the deck and ran down the short companionway. The older man had put Geean in one of the bunks, and Lennar and Harld on the cabin floor. Treece was in the other bunk and Somerville was leaning over her while he adjusted the pillow. She was smiling up at him, but he appeared not to notice.

Tarrant moved quietly in behind him, brushed his supporting left arm out of the way and threw his weight on Somerville's back. Somerville collapsed on to Treece with a startled curse which was stifled as she clamped her open mouth to his. He struggled for a moment, then his body relaxed. Tarrant stepped back and allowed him to regain his feet.

"There's no point in aiming for the Bergmann transceivers themselves," Somerville said at once. "There could be as many as a dozen of them all around the world, and even if we could get to them quickly—which we can't—they're bound to be fairly indestructible."

"You're saying it's hopeless?"

Somerville shook his head. "I'm saying that particular approach is hopeless."

"What do we do, then?"

"I think we should refer back to the old master himself." Somerville took off his bandana and wiped perspiration from his neck with it as he stepped over Lennar's and Harld's outstretched legs to reach his book-shelf. "Would you like to bring Myrah down out of the heat? We don't want to lose any units through sunstroke."

"Okay." Tarrant went up on deck, lifted Myrah bodily and carried her down into the crowded cabin. Neither of them spoke during the process, and when he set her on the floor between Lennar and Harld she lay back with complete passivity.

"I haven't any Swedish," Somerville said, spreading a book on his chart table, "but this is supposed to be a good translation of Bergmann's original *Balance of Life*. It was written five years before he died, which was about the time the history books say dysteleonic radiation was discovered, but listen to this."

Somerville cleared his throat and began to read. "The advantages of dysteleonic radiation for communications and power transmission would be that there would be virtually no transmission losses over global distances; the beams would be undetectable to all but the most advanced technological cultures; and, finally, they would be immune to interference. Barring the possibility that the hydrospheric balance valves are energised and controlled through a medium of such sophistication that we are unable even to guess at its nature, one must conclude that dysteleonics are employed for this purpose.

"I predict that in the near future, provided that our civilisation emerges intact from its present crisis, men will learn routinely to generate and detect dysteleonic radiation. And when they do they will discover they are not breaking new ground, but merely following in the footsteps of that ancient race to which I have given the name of Paleotechs. And the irrefutable evidence will be all about them in the form of beams of dysteleonic radiation linking the Earth's hydrospheric balance valves to their central energising and control station."

Somerville set the book down on the table. "What do you think of that?"

Tarrant shrugged. "Quite a lot of evangelistic fervour, but where does it get us?"

"Bergmann went on to postulate that his control station would be positioned on the equator and somewhere near the centre of the Earth's largest ocean—which means it isn't all that far from here. Anybody who could...."

"Wait a minute!" Tarrant snapped his fingers. "There was something about dysteleonics when I was in the Air Force! Seven or eight years ago, it was. One of the men in my squadron was put on escort duty and he did a couple of runs up to Baker Island with a Department of Science turbojet. He had no idea why the top brass thought the missions were so important, but he picked up the word dysteleonics."

"On Baker Island itself, was it?"

"Yes. *No!* There was a small island a hundred kilometres or so to the east. It had an odd sort of a name."

"Harpoon?"

"That's it. How did you know?"

Somerville sighed as he closed up his book and put it back on the shelf. "It would have saved me a hell of a lot of money and time if we'd got together years ago. Why didn't you tell me you were in the South Newzealand Air Force?"

"It's a bit tricky—I'm still supposed to be in it."

"I see." Somerville tied his bandana around his balding head again. "Let's go up on deck—it's time we were on our way back to the island."

Oblivious of the watchful gazes of the five other humans, Tarrant followed Somerville up the steps and into the bright, simplistic universe of green ocean and blue sky. A slight breeze had sprung up and Tarrant's boat was nuzzling *The Rose of York* like a calf seeking milk from a cow.

"What was all that about saving you time and money?" he said.

Somerville untied Tarrant's boat and began walking with it to the stern of his own boat in preparation for towing. "I've been interested in this Bergmann thing for more than ten years. A couple of years ago I even went to Brisbane and bought myself some time on what's left of the Oceania computer. Most of it is dead, or electronically gangrenous, and all the links west of Celebes are suspect. It did a kind of search and analysis, though—and indicated a spread of islets and atolls all the way out to the Low Archipelago. Harpoon was one of them."

Tarrant blinked at him. "You were lucky to get that much. I mean, what does it know about Bergmann's Hypothesis?"

"I didn't ask about Bergmann. I was working on reports of unusual military activity, furtive scientific expeditions, compass anomalies—dysteleonic radiation does that, you know. That sort of thing." Somerville glanced up from hitching the smaller boat to his stern post. "There I was in Brisbane wasting three months' profits, and you were back here sitting on the facts I needed."

"Not really," Tarrant said. "I'd forgotten all about it. I didn't even know the pilot who went up there, and I only heard him mention it once in the mess." He pressed a hand to the right side of his chest. "I must have had some assistance."

Somerville nodded seriously, momentarily touching his own chest. "It would be a double tragedy if we couldn't save Ka. Obviously his life has to be preserved at all costs, but on top of that there's the benefit he could bring to other people besides us."

Tarrant tried to imagine an existence without the companionship of the sentient black jelly which nestled within his right lung, feeding its messages of comfort directly into his nervous system. He drew back from the bleak prospect, and the desperate urgency of the situation began to bear down on him.

"Will," he said, gripping the older man's shoulder, "let's assume there's some kind of control station on Harpoon Island. It's bound to be way down below the surface. We wouldn't be able to touch it, let alone put it out of action, unless we had something like...."

"A tactical nuke?"

"That's right."

Somerville grinned his piratical grin. "There's one back on Cawley Island. Three, in fact."

Tarrant had to make an effort to prevent his jaw sagging. "What are you saying, Will?"

"It's true—that's one of the reasons we're going back there."

"But where did they come from? Who has them?"

"Don't forget the farm's been in existence for almost forty years," Somerville said, "and things weren't so secure around here at first. Spiegel was still raiding out of the New Hebrides, King Tom out of Suva, and the Barrett brothers out of New Caledonia. Into the bargain there was always the chance of pirates coming along and cleaning the place out—food was a lot scarcer in those days, and a shipload of protein cake was worth a fortune.

"When old Patch Cawley and the others settled here to start the farm he had a Mark 89 mortar with him—stolen from a Peruvian sub-killer—and three general purpose nuclear loads for it. He was fully prepared to let fly if anybody had shown up to make trouble, but nothing ever happened. Maybe the word got around. Anyway, the stuff is still there."

"Nobody told me about it," Tarrant said.

"It isn't supposed to be general knowledge, though I imagine nearly every independent island has something similar tucked away. Nobody but members of the Inner Council are told officially, and they're the only ones who have access to it."

"Do you know where it is?"

Somerville looked surprised at the question. "Of course! Come on—let's get back."

Tarrant went with him to the upper deck and leaned on a rail while Somerville switched on his motors and swung the cruiser around to the south. *The Rose of York* had much more space for solar panel arrays and batteries, and therefore was faster than Tarrant's nameless boat in spite of the extra weight. Tarrant watched its bow wave build up on each side and wondered if it was fast enough to out-distance the remaining big squid, the creature he now knew as the Horra. As the farm came into view ahead—a thin white line of booms, topped by a band of vivid green and the misty blue triangle of the island—he fetched his rifle and began scanning the water In the clear light of the late afternoon he could see a considerable distance below the surface.

Somerville glanced over his shoulder. "What are you looking for?"

"Horra. This might sound crazy, Will—but I think I recognised the big one which nearly capsized my boat."

"You think it might be following us?"

"I'm not sure. It seems malicious enough, but could it be that intelligent?"

"Wouldn't be surprised." Somerville locked the wheel and took a bundle of black cheroots from his shirt pocket. "The reason I came out to see you earlier on was that I had never seen a cellular structure anything like theirs before. My microscope was too small for the job, but the plasma membranes seemed to have an extra layer."

"Would that lead to an increase in intelligence?"

"I couldn't answer that." Somerville put a cheroot in his mouth and took out his lighter. "But squid and octopus are fairly intelligent to start off with, and when you have a viable mutation which leads to a big increase in size—coupled with extra cell complexity—anything could happen."

Somerville lit the cheroot, inhaled deeply and a curious expression appeared on his face. He blew the smoke out immediately, clutching his right side, then stamped out the cheroot and threw the rest of the bundle overboard.

The tomb of Captain Patch Cawley was in a small memorial garden on the island's central peak.

It was an appropriate place for the storage of the community's small arsenal—those who were in on the secret thought of him as still keeping his finger on the trigger—and it had the advantage of being easy to secure. The fact that the vault was always locked excited no comment, and even the most adventurous of the island's young people had no desire to pry inside. There was the additional advantage that the site provided 360-degree coverage of the surrounding sea, making it possible for a trained man to drop a nuclear shell into the midst of an invading fleet regardless of the direction from which it came. After decades of peace, however, this consideration had begun to seem more and more academic, and the garden remained a focus of tranquillity for those who liked to sit on its stone benches and admire the panoramic views.

Tarrant and Somerville crouched in the darkness among the trees and watched the quiet scene. They had spent the latter part of the afternoon and the early evening in obtaining supplies and loading them on to *The Rose of York*. As darkness had approached they had come up the hill by separate routes, only to find a middle-aged couple and two boys of about ten sitting in the garden opposite the door of the vault. The man was peacefully smoking a cigarette, the woman was talking to him with quiet concentration, and the boys were playing a game with white pebbles.

"They look like being there all night," Tarrant said in a low voice. "What are we going to do?"

Somerville raised his shoulders. "We might have to kill them."

Tarrant shook his head. "I thought of that, but the bodies could be found at any time—and we can't afford to be at the centre of a manhunt."

"We could put them in the vault."

Tarrant evaluated the situation and calculated that several days were likely to elapse before anybody went near the door of the vault. "That seems all right. We'll need to go for the kids first, because they can run faster—then I'll take the man and you can deal with the woman."

He took his knife from its sheath and signalled for Somerville to follow him as he moved off through the foliage to get nearer the family.

"Wait a minute," Somerville said. "I think they're...." He

parted the wall of shrubs with his hand and they watched as the man stubbed out his cigarette and got to his feet. The woman stood up with him and they walked towards the garden's west gate, leaving the boys still absorbed in their game. At the gate the man turned and called the children. They gathered up the pebbles and ran to him, laughing, each trying to hold the other back.

"Just as well," Tarrant said, putting his knife away. "There might have been too much noise."

The two men waited in concealment for another minute before crossing the garden. Both had crowbars hidden beneath their jackets, and under their combined assault the panelled wooden door of the tomb opened almost at once. They went inside and closed the door behind them. Somerville switched on a small flashlight and its beam picked out a simple sarcophagus in the middle of the circular building. The air was dry and faintly spicy, a smell which Tarrant found evocative of death and the slow-gathering dust of eternity. He was grateful for the reassuring presence within his ribcage, the reminder that he was no longer alone, no longer subject to the mortality of the individual.

The wavering spot of light jumped to a wooden partition which cut off a segment of the room. Attempts had been made to have the partition blend with the architecture, but the effect was spoiled by an incongruous bolt and padlock on the central door. Tarrant prised the lock off and opened the door to reveal the squat shape of a 500-millimetre mortar beneath a plastic cover. Behind it, resting in low cradles, were three red-and-white striped cylinders with built-in carrying handles.

"That's handy—they're still in the ready-use canisters," Tarrant said. "I was afraid they might be already hooked up to propellent charges."

"I don't think there are any propellents. They would have become unstable a long time ago, and nobody has bothered to get new stuff." Somerville shone his light around the equipment shelves and lifted a pouch of specialised tools and crammed it into his jacket pocket. "That's all—let's go."

They picked up one of the heavy plastic canisters between them and carried it out of the vault. Tarrant closed the doors and pressed the splintered wood of the edges back into place. The night sky was opulent with stars, and Venus was burning low in the west, a steel-white flare so bright that it scribed a line of silver on the ocean. Somerville took off his jacket and draped it over the canister to hide the garish markings, and they set off walking down the hill. They met nobody in the quiet, sloping avenues, there being no sign of life on the island but for the windows which glowed lemon and white and amber among the trees.

The bomb was heavier than Tarrant had anticipated, but in spite of frequent pauses they got it to the boat in less than an hour. They stowed it in a rope locker, and Somerville went below to tend to the five castaways and prepare a meal, entrusting Tarrant with the job of taking them out to sea by way of the north channel. The boat rode quietly between the twin lines of marker globes, with Tarrant's boat on tow, breasting the scented and oxygen-rich air which lay over the farm in an invisible blanket. About halfway to the rim Somerville emerged from below deck with a tray of food which he handed to Tarrant before taking over the wheel.

"How is it down there?" Tarrant said, sipping some of the rum which his host dispensed in the same way that others poured coffee.

"Hot." Somerville opened his white shirt to the waist. "Young Geean seems a lot better already, though. First exposure to antibiotics and all that."

"Can they move around?"

"Not much. Ideally they should be in something like a shallow pool—out of the water it's quite a strain for them even to move their arms. I'd say that if they hadn't been very active up there, wherever it is, they couldn't have made it in our gravity at all."

Tarrant stared into the night sky for a moment. "Is it worth all the trouble to keep them alive?"

"We'll have to see," Somerville replied. "Perhaps for recruiting other help."

"Okay." Tarrant ate sparingly from the bread, fruit and nuts on his tray, and finished off the beaker of rum. "I think I'll get a few hours of sleep up here."

He lay down on the bench seat at the side of the upper deck. It had been a long and tiring day, and he expected to fall asleep almost at once, but the spirit he had drunk was curling warmly in his veins, triggering responses in his autonomic nerve system. All the heat of his body, all the strength and all the blood, seemed to migrate to his genitals, producing a painful, insistent tumescence. After ten restless minutes he sat up.

"It's no use," he said. "I won't be able to sleep until I get rid of this."

Somerville kept his gaze straight ahead. "You know where the women are, old son."

Tarrant nodded. He stood up and went towards the head of the companionway, unbuttoning his pants as he walked. The hot air rising from the cabin carried with it the mingled odours of hair, perspiration and human flesh, further stimulating his physical craving. He entered the cabin without speaking. Somerville had left a small globe burning, and the first person Tarrant saw by its faint light was the older woman, Treece, lying in the starboard bunk.

"You'll do," he said unemotionally, casually, going straight to her.

123

# CHAPTER TWELVE

*The Rose of York* was fitted with a satellite navigation system which had been guaranteed by its manufacturers to be an exact duplicate of a type perfected three centuries earlier. Their literature had stated that the quality and reliability were as good as in the original hardware, but Somerville had never been able to check on that claim because the most vulnerable part of the system—the satellites themselves—had begun functioning erratically soon after he acquired the boat. He had been forced to devise a hybrid technique for getting around the South Pacific, a method using traditional dead reckoning, radio beacons where available, and the occasional flash of lucidity from his satnav equipment.

Tarrant had become accustomed to similar makeshifts on a more sophisticated level in his flying days, and he quickly learned all that was necessary to navigate the boat. Somerville and he took four-hour spells at the wheel throughout the first night and the following day, mainly to monitor the self-steering gear. Between daytime watches Tarrant sat at the stern with his rifle cradled in his lap. His own boat was following the larger one, duckling fashion, and he kept a close watch on the water all around it, hoping to see a familiar mottled shape come to the surface. He could not say if he was going by instinct, or receiving guidance from the friend he carried within his chest, but he was certain the big squid was not far away. And he would be unable to work comfortably in the water until he had seen the huge body ripped into streamers and drifting with the tide.

At other times he went below and attended to chores such as helping the three women and two men to reach the cruiser's chemical lavatory. Without the pressures of sexual deprivation, he handled the men and women impartially, and there was no conversation with them at any time. He understood, and was proud, that Ka regarded Somerville and him as superior instruments of his will. They were far stronger than the people of the Clan, mobile, possessed of valuable skills and knowledge—and as such had no reason to communicate with any but each other. The five he had rescued from the water had been useful in that they had served to induct Somerville and him into the corporate entity that was Ka, and they might be useful again, but until then they were relegated to the status of inert appendages.

Several times during the day they saw other craft. At one point a destroyer flying the Republic of Queensland flag came almost to within hailing distance, but drew away incuriously to dwindle over the horizon. Sunset found *The Rose of York* holding its north-easterly course in a calm, glassy sea which progressively darkened from green to black as the light faded from the sky. When Tarrant went up for his spell of duty he discovered Somerville anxiously examining the meters which reported the state of the boat's propulsion system.

"We're down about eight volts," Somerville said gloomily. "Some of the batteries aren't holding their charges."

"It may not come to much." Tarrant insinuated his flat body into the space beside Somerville and clicked switches which isolated various battery trays, his eyes taking in the condition of each. On one circuit the meter needles sagged dramatically. "There's where the trouble is—Port Four."

Somerville swore savagely. "I only bought that set last month. It's the same old story—new is bad."

"Let's just wait and see what happens," Tarrant said. "They may not collapse for days."

At regular intervals during the next four hours he ran checks on the suspect tray and was forced to admit that the overall condition of the batteries in Port Four was deteriorating at a noticeable rate. The boat continued to cut its way through the darkness, using energy its solar panels had

125

gathered and fed into the batteries during the day, but its speed was gradually falling. Tarrant knew he would soon have to choose between selecting a lower propeller speed or risking the consequences of overloading the remaining healthy units.

"We can't afford to lose speed," Somerville said when he came back on watch.

"It'll only be for a couple of hours." Tarrant glanced at his watch. "At first light we can bring my boat alongside and transfer my batteries."

Somerville came to decision. "We'll do that right now, without waiting for first light—I want those batteries on charge as soon as the sun comes up."

Tarrant nodded compliantly and, leaving the boat to steer itself, they went aft. It took only a few minutes to haul the smaller boat alongside against the drag of the bow wave. As Tarrant climbed down into it, stretching his legs across a margin of racing black water, he felt a moment of uneasiness. It seemed to him that he had once known a good reason to avoid that kind of situation, but in the urgency of the moment he had forgotten what it could be. In any case, no harm could befall him as long as his friend and mentor quivered within his chest cavity. He ran a line up from the stern of his boat and Somerville secured it, creating a more stable bond between the two craft.

The task of transferring the batteries was longer and more difficult than Tarrant had expected. In the past he had done similar work without paying too much attention to wisps of gas in the battery compartment, but now each time he put his head in too far he felt a strange, writhing pain in his right lung and was forced to draw back. The batteries themselves were tricky to disconnect in the uncertain light from Somerville's lamp, and became wilfully massive as they were being handed from one boat to the other, causing strained muscles and broken fingernails.

Tarrant was sweating profusely by the time he had passed over the last weighty cube and his arms were trembling with fatigue. His boat was riding higher in the water, testimony to the amount of work he had done, and with the change in angle of the connecting ropes had moved a short distance away from *The Rose of York*. Tarrant knelt down to replace the cover of his battery compartment. He was leaning forward, tightening wing nuts, when the cruiser gave his boat a sharp nudge, and he fell forward against the outer gunwale. In the same instant something wet and dark slapped itself around his waist. Then he was in the water, facing death by nightmare.

Other tentacles encircled his body as he went below the surface. Guided by instincts that had never been called into play before, Tarrant twisted violently, trying to get his booted feet into the central mouth area towards which he was being drawn. His feet bedded on a rubbery mass. Mercifully, there was no crushing pain which would have let him know he had driven his feet into the squid's mouth, but his situation was nonetheless critical. He was under water, in the grip of a monster which thrived in that environment, and being carried further downward with every second. In a very short time the air in his lungs would be exhausted and he would drown, provided that the Horra—using all its advantages—had not managed to destroy him first.

As Tarrant fought to retain his meagre supply of air against the fierce pressure on his chest, he became aware of yet another threat to his life. One of the squid's tentacles, smoother than the others, was feeling for his mouth, trying to force its way into his throat. He got his right hand free from the coils which were gathering around his body and fended off the stabbing arm, but he knew his success had to be pitifully brief. The dead air in his chest was trying to explode outwards, creating a force which could be resisted for only a matter of seconds. As the blood-warm bubbles began to flee from his nostrils, Tarrant experienced a sense of resignation, discovered that death was only terrible while one refused to accept its inevitability. His struggles began to weaken as he realised that a being which had to breathe air would never be a match for one which spent its entire existence under water.

He relaxed, already partially drowned, waiting for the inevitable—then became aware of the steady pulsing of water at his right leg. It was the pumping action of the squid's siphon. Part of his mind noted the phenomenon and was unconcerned, but another part—which housed all that was stubborn and unyielding in Tarrant's character—saw it as searing revelation. The squid, just like any other animal, *did* have to breathe, *did* rely on oxygen to keep it alive. And to that extent it was every bit as vulnerable as he.

Summoning the last remnants of his strength, he moved his right foot sideways. It encountered the leathery, penis-like tube of the Horra's siphon at full extent as it exhaled water. He waited until the tube had retracted then thrust his foot down inside it. The effect on the creature was immediate. It convulsed and swerved and tumbled, and the tentacles which had been drawing Tarrant inwards relaxed their hold and began pushing him away. As this was something they had not been designed to do, they were relatively ineffectual, and Tarrant—aware he could not survive a fresh attack—fought to remain inside the cone of threshing arms. The air bubbles streamed from his mouth and nose, shivering and scrambling in their eagerness to fly to the surface.

There was an indeterminate period—a flashing of lights, the thunder of organic pumps—during which Tarrant felt nothing but a dark satisfaction that he had not been an easy prey; then he was forced to open his mouth and let himself be invaded by the sea. . . .

"*. . . Never seen anything like . . . thought it was some kind of leech, but the . . . seems to be a complete lack of specialised organs. . . .*"

The voices came and went for a long time, meaningless as the drone of bees on a summer afternoon.

Tarrant opened his eyes and saw a flat, whitish plain crossed by parallel black canals which receded into infinity. Here and there on the Dali landscape were monstrous objects which might have resembled shoes but for their enormous size. He became aware of a weight on his back, of the insistent pressure of hands. At first he accepted the incomprehensible new world without question, suffused with a vague relief at being able to see or feel anything, then one of the shoe-like things moved and he knew he was lying with his face pressed against the wooden deck of a ship. He tried to speak, but renewed pressure on his back turned the unborn words into a rasping moan.

"We've got him," a man's voice said. "For a while I didn't think he was going to make it."

With the return of consciousness, the natural mechanisms of coughing and retching took over the job of expelling water from Tarrant's body and he gave himself up to it for minute after minute. Finally the muscular spasms began to ease, and the authoritative voice spoke again.

"Wrap those blankets around him and take him inside. Get some hot coffee into him." There was a pause. "And bring that bucket with you."

Tarrant was lifted and carried across the deck, during which process he glimpsed naval grey superstructure, a broad up-raised bow reminiscent of that of a trawler, and a distant golden fire on the horizon which told him the sun was rising. He was taken into a spacious deck-house and placed in a chair. In spite of the predominant battleship grey, the men who carried him were wearing an assortment of lightweight civilian clothes. The senior man wore an officer's peaked cap, but with a careless jauntiness which—in conjunction with his loose red shirt and open sandals—made him look like a week-end sailor. He was a stoop-shouldered man in his fifties, with crisp waves of greying hair, steel-rimmed glasses and a look of quizzical intelligence.

Tarrant watched him blankly over the rim of the mug which was being held to his lips, and tried to drag himself fully into the present moment. He liked this man who was standing before him, he liked the feeling of being cared for, he liked the warm and dry airiness of the deck-house ... but bad things had been happening to him, something terrible had come into his life. Tarrant let his gaze rove around, taking in the watchful faces, the profusion of electronic equipment on shelves and benches, the white plastic bucket on the deck near his feet, the eel-like sliver of black jelly which lay in the bottom of the bucket. . . .

"Kill it!" he screamed, throwing himself forward. "Kill that thing! *Kill it!*"

"Take it easy, son." Strong hands pushed him back into his chair and held him immobile.

"Burn it," Tarrant pleaded. "Do you hear me? I want it dead!" He renewed his struggles to get out of the chair, but in his weakened condition the others contained him easily. Tarrant began to sob.

"That thing was *inside* me, for God's sake! It made me . . ." As his memory returned in full, he doubled forward in a paroxysm of nausea, and coffee spurted from his mouth on to the deck.

"Take the bucket out of his sight," the senior man ordered, "but be careful with it."

When the bucket was carried away Tarrant slumped back in his chair. "Thank you, thank you—but don't let anybody touch it. Don't let it get near anybody's mouth, because if you do . . ."

His jaw clamped and tears welled into his eyes as he recalled some of the horrors of his Ka-existence. He had been prepared to kill a whole family to gain perhaps an hour, and the people, the children, had been *nothing* to him. He had been more inhuman than the Horra themselves. He had left two nuclear weapons in an unlocked building, where they could be found and tampered with by children. And there had been other things. Using a helpless woman like a. . . . Tarrant gave a deep sigh and huddled himself up in the blankets, rocking from side to side in the chair.

"I'm Theo Martine," the grey-haired man said, gripping Tarrant's shoulders and holding him steady. "And this is a research vessel of the South Newzealand Navy. What's your name?"

"Hal Tarrant."

"What were you doing in the sea? Did you go overboard from a ship?"

Tarrant shook his head and almost managed to smile. "You'll never believe me."

"Try me."

"It's no use, I tell you."

Martine's face became less kindly, more determined. "This isn't getting us anywhere. Would it help you if I told you that the squid we picked up along with you is like nothing else on this Earth? And that you owe your life to that fact?"

"In what way?" Tarrant said cautiously.

"It's an outsize version of the common squid, which is a nektonic-pelagic animal. All nektonic species are slightly heavier than water, which means that when they die they sink to the bottom. The one you managed to kill floated to the surface, bringing you with it, so I knew immediately that giantism wasn't its only peculiarity. Things like that intrigue me, Mr Tarrant. And things like that mobile jelly we pumped out of your lungs intrigue me even more, so I want you to start telling me what you know about them. All right?"

Tarrant nodded, his mind plagued by doubts, then a new thought occurred to him. Will Somerville, Myrah, Lennar and the others were on their way to Harpoon Island with the intention of exploding a nuclear bomb on it. Detonating such a bomb was a fairly straightforward matter for a man with military experience, but because it was intended for artillery use the maximum delay available on the fuse circuits varied from only thirty to sixty seconds, depending on the type of weapon. This consideration had not troubled Tarrant while he was aboard *The Rose of York*, and he understood now that Ka had suppressed it. Somerville still had that lethal blind spot, and therefore he was going to his death—as were the group of lost, hag-ridden men and women travelling with him.

"Big decision?" Martine said.

"Not really." Tarrant met his gaze squarely. "Does the name Ulrich Bergmann mean anything to you?" He saw the muscles of Martine's face sag momentarily.

"Just a minute," Martine said briskly, making an immediate recovery. He turned to the small group of men who were with him. "I'm taking Mr Tarrant to my room, where he can rest properly. In the meantime I want that squid sectioned and examined. Keep an eye on the other thing and let me know if it shows any sign of change."

Martine helped Tarrant to his feet. They went aft, climbed a flight of steps and entered a roomy cabin which was furnished as living quarters. Martine handed Tarrant a towel, then opened a drawer and passed him clean underwear, a shirt and a pair of shorts. As he moved about the cabin his eyes watched Tarrant unblinkingly.

"I did tell you," he said finally, "that this is a ship of the South Newzealand Navy."

"You did." Tarrant began to dry his hair with the towel. His arms felt weak, difficult to control.

"You sound like a Newzealander yourself."

"I am." Tarrant began to wonder where the interview was leading.

"North or South?"

"South. I was born in Dunedin."

"Can you prove that?"

"Not right now—all my papers are at my home on Cawley Island."

"So you can't prove you're not a spy?" Martine had ceased looking like an amateur yachtsman, and was craning forward with his head tilted for Tarrant's reply.

"A *spy*?" Tarrant looked at him in astonishment. "What would a spy be doing out here in the middle of ... ?"

"You were the one who mentioned Bergmann," Martine cut in.

Tarrant recalled his country's interest in Harpoon Island seven years earlier and half-formed ideas began to stir in his mind. "Look," he said, "if I was snooping on your research into dysteleonics I wouldn't come right out and say it, would I?"

Martine gave an unexpected laugh. "If that sort of reasoning was valid anybody who was caught doing anything, anywhere, would only have to mention his crime first, and thus prove his innocence."

"I haven't committed any crime."

"Then perhaps you'll tell me what you have been doing."

"I guess I'd better." Tarrant, having decided on complete honesty, led off with a brief sketch of his service career and his desertion from the South Newzealand Air Force. While he was changing into the dry clothes Martine had provided, he described the events of the past few days, beginning with his first brush with the Horra and ending with his being plucked overboard from his boat. The account took twenty minutes, but Martine heard him out with no interruptions, although at times he grew distinctly restless.

"You said earlier that you hadn't committed any crime," Martine commented after a lengthy pause. "What about this nuclear mortar bomb you took?"

"*I* didn't take it—I've explained to you that I had no moral responsibility." Tarrant's concern about the two bombs remaining on Cawley Island came back to him. "I'd like you to put a signal through to the chairman of the Inner Council on Cawley and let him know the armoury isn't secure."

"I'll do that, but right now I'm worried about the third bomb—the one your friend has." Martine squeezed his lower lip between finger and thumb, his eyes hard on Tarrant's. "You see, we have nearly twenty people on Harpoon Island, and—from what you say—Mr Somerville would have no compunction about wiping them out."

Tarrant shook his head impatiently. "I tell you it isn't Will Somerville who ... What are your people doing on Harpoon?"

"I shouldn't tell you, but you've given me some valuable information...." Martine's face relaxed slightly. "They're excavating for the machine."

"Then it *is* there. Will was right!"

"There's something down there. We haven't been able to

measure its size or depth. The amount of dysteleonics activity in the area makes nonsense of all our readings. That's the trouble with this stuff—above a certain intensity it makes compasses and most other instruments go haywire, but once it drops below a threshold level we can't even detect it." Martine's eyes glistened as he warmed to his subject. "We've got to have dysteleonics—it's the only way we'll ever get the *per capita* energy quota back up to 21st century levels—but progress has been so slow.

"Would you believe that picking you out of the water this morning, a chance find if ever there was one, has advanced our work by six months or a year?"

"In what way?" Tarrant felt exhausted and had a pounding headache, but his mind had never been so alert.

"There must be a Bergmann transceiver just north of Cawley Island, so—for the first time—we can draw a line on a map and know it represents a dysteleonics beam."

"That's good," Tarrant said. "I'm glad about that—but what are you going to do about Will Somerville and the others?"

"There's only one thing I can do." Martine blinked mildly behind his glasses. "I have to turn the matter over to the military and have them stopped."

'When I was with Interceptor Command," Tarrant said thoughtfully, "there was a very strict policy for dealing with nuclear threats, even tactical stuff."

"I'm not a military man," Martine replied, "but I can see the need for such a policy. I'm sorry."

"But they don't deserve to be killed."

Martine walked around the room before answering. "There's more at stake than the lives of the twenty people on Harpoon, though in my opinion that issue alone justifies the use of maximum force against Somerville. There's more at stake than the South Newzealand dysteleonics research programme. We've made the rather humbling discovery that human life on this planet has been artificially nurtured for millennia, and now that we know about the system of balances we have to protect it or bear the full brunt of future climatic changes.

"There could be millions of lives at stake here, billions of lives—and that's why your friend Somerville has to be stopped before he gets anywhere near that machine. He's a threat to the future of the whole race."

Tarrant leaned forward, gripping the arms of his chair. "I keep telling you it isn't Will Somerville who's the enemy. He and the others have no control over their actions."

"Even if that were true, the situation remains effectively the same."

Tarrant was taken by surprise. "Don't you believe me?"

"Look at it from my point of view," Martine said reasonably. "A week ago would you have believed in a mutated medusa-fish with telepathic powers? One which can exert control over animals and human beings?"

"But you believed everything else, didn't you? I mean, a planetoid made up of sea water is a pretty unlikely...."

"That's different," Martine interrupted. "I already knew about the planetoid."

Tarrant looked at him in surprise. "How?"

"We located it by telescope and long-range radar more than two years ago. In fact, we found two planetoids in the same orbit, between Earth and Venus."

"I see." Tarrant began to appreciate the extent of the South Newzealand investigations. "And naturally you didn't tell anybody?"

"Of course not. That information is all part of a single matrix."

Tarrant cradled his head in his hands for a moment, trying to fight off his pain and tiredness. "Have you a drink? Anything alcoholic?"

Martine went to a wall locker and came back with a glass of brandy. "I'll leave you to work on that while I go to the radio room." His voice was quiet but firm. "I can't delay that message any longer."

He went out and closed the door behind him. Before the door had completely shut Tarrant saw him begin to speak to someone in the corridor outside, and knew he was under guard. He sipped the brandy and thought about Will Somerville sailing his boat towards a death which was now doubly certain. The others deserved a better fate, too. It filled Tarrant with a peculiar anguish to think of Myrah, in particular, living her grim travesty of a normal life for more than twenty years, then going through the enormity of a marriage to Ka, and surviving the transit to Earth—only to be obliterated by an air-to-surface rocket or a homing torpedo. He would have to renew his efforts to persuade Martine to stay his hand, even if it was only to gain a little breathing space.

"That's that," Martine said, coming back into the room. "They're checking with Cawley Island to confirm that a nuclear mortar has been taken, then the hunt will be on. Incidentally, somebody on Cawley is going to get a roasting for possessing those things."

"To hell with them," Tarrant snapped. "Look, Captain, is it the ...?"

"I'm not actually a naval officer," Martine interrupted. "I don't even know how to drive this ship. I'm a Principal Science Officer with the Marine Technology Board."

"Sorry. I didn't realise."

"It doesn't matter." Martine gave him a twinkly, penetrating glance. "Go on, Mr Tarrant—I believe you were going to try convincing me that telepathy is an established fact."

Tarrant nodded. "It may not be an established fact, but we might be able to establish it to your satisfaction in a few minutes."

"What would be the point?"

"Well, if I can get you to accept direct transference of data, it's only a short step to believing in a mental transmitter so powerful that it swamps out everything else in the receiver's brain."

"A short step for you perhaps, but a great leap for a scientist." Martine looked over his glasses. "How would you do it, anyway?"

"You've still got that tissue you pumped out of my lungs?"

"It doesn't prove anything—new marine life forms are still being found every year."

"Yes, but if you divide it in two, and put the two parts in separate rooms, you've only to do something to one part...."

"And see if the other part reacts!" Martine went to the locker and poured some brandy for himself, once again playing the part of the jaunty amateur sailor. "You propose doing something fairly drastic to the first half?"

"For the purpose of the experiment," Tarrant said, "there's no point in tickling it."

Fifteen minutes later he was standing in a small chemical laboratory on a lower deck of the ship. He had almost conquered his first blind reaction to the sight of the Ka tissue, but his stomach heaved intermittently as he watched the movements of the egg-sized gob of black jelly. The entire organism had been poured out of the bucket and divided in two by pressing down on it with a metal sheet. Both halves had then been scooped into glass jars. One of them was in Martine's quarters on the upper deck and the other had been taken to the laboratory by Tarrant. Wet highlights glistened on its surface as it furled and flattened, restlessly exploring its surroundings with pseudopods which sometimes extended right across the container. When it managed to rise a short distance up the side of the jar its undersurface was seen to have the dark redness of clotted blood.

"Pleasant little fellow," Tarrant's companion said. He was a bearded young research assistant who had been introduced to Tarrant as Les Anvers.

"A real charmer." Tarrant tried to sound emotionless as he took the stopper off the bottle of concentrated hydrochloric acid which had been provided by Martine. "Give the word at any time."

Anvers glanced reluctantly at his stopwatch and then at Tarrant. "I don't like doing this to anything that's alive."

"I'm the one that's doing it," Tarrant told him. "Say when."

Anvers shrugged, waited a short time, then stopped the watch. "Now!"

Tarrant immediately poured the acid into the jar and watched, his mouth twitching uncontrollably, as the black jelly writhed in the swiftly darkening fluid. In a matter of seconds there was nothing left but a foul-smelling organic slurry on the surface of which bubbles clustered like a swarming of blood-red beetles. Appalled though he was, Tarrant felt a deep pang of satisfaction. *I hope that got home to you, Ka,* he thought. *I hope you felt that.* He became aware that Anvers was staring at him.

"It's all in a good cause," he said, realising the futility of trying to explain what had been happening, that he was trying to save the lives of men and women.

Anvers nodded without speaking and placed a square of glass on the jar to contain the fumes which were rising from it. A minute later Martine came into the laboratory carrying his own stopwatch. He took the other watch from Anders and waited until the assistant had gone out before comparing the two readings. They were the same to within a fraction of a second.

"There was a marked reaction," he said. "The control specimen seemed to go mad."

Tarrant nodded peacefully. "I'm glad about that."

Martine looked away from him. "This place stinks."

"If you want to be squeamish," Tarrant said, angered, "be squeamish about those people who are carrying that stuff around inside them. You don't like this experiment? All right—I'll suggest a better one. Take that other piece of tissue and put it on your tongue and see what happens. Why don't we go up there right now?"

"You've made your point," Martine said. "Don't overdo it."

Tarrant bunched his fists in exasperation. "I'm sorry, but nobody *understands*—and there's so little time. How long do you think it will take them to find Somerville's boat?"

"Three or four days if he's lucky."

"That long? I don't get it."

"It appears," Martine said drily, "that all our long-range,

138

all-weather, day-and-night reconnaissance aircraft are grounded because the engines have started to fall off them. Perhaps you encountered similar problems in your flying days?"

"All the time—but what about the Navy?"

"They've got two destroyers in operational condition, and both are going straight to Harpoon Island. The idea must be to wait there until your friend shows up. I'm told that one of them is equipped with fairly reliable homing missiles, so...."

Tarrant understood how Martine had arrived at his estimate of the time until Somerville would be intercepted—that was how long it would take *The Rose of York* to reach the vicinity of Harpoon Island. Even in the 20th century it had been common for complex warships to spend half their lifetimes in dock, and the South Newzealand Admiralty was grandiosely trying to operate a similar type of vessel—with the result that as many as eight out of ten vessels would be laid up for scheduled and unscheduled repairs at any given time. This loss of technical competence was giving Somerville a brief respite, but it was nothing more than a stay of execution. Commanders who were armed with weapons they could not fully trust would employ the tactics of instantaneous overkill.

"Look," Tarrant said desperately, "why don't we go after Somerville in this ship?"

"That's out of the question."

"I don't see why. If we start from the area where you picked me up, we can calculate Somerville's course and...." Tarrant broke off as he saw that the geniality had faded from Martine's face.

"You don't seem to appreciate your position in this affair," Martine said. "It's serious enough that you're a deserter from the Air Force, but being an accomplice in the theft of a nuclear device makes you an international criminal." He held up one hand to forestall Tarrant's protest.

"It doesn't matter that I personally am beginning to believe you had no control over your actions—I have to obey the orders I received from Christchurch. And that means I have to place you under arrest and take you to the authorities."

"You wouldn't do that," Tarrant challenged unthinkingly.

Martine looked surprised, then opened the door and nodded to someone outside. Two men with the brown, vein-corded forearms of deckhands moved into view. They were of medium size and build, but something in the half-expectant way they looked at Tarrant told him they had been selected for their ability to deal with trouble.

"I'm supposed to lock you in a store room, but I don't want to do that," Martine said. "Instead I'm putting you in an ordinary cabin on this deck. The door won't be locked, but there'll be a guard on it at all times and you'll be doing yourself a favour if you don't try to get away. If you co-operate in this arrangement I'm sure you'll be very comfortable."

"Thanks a lot." Tarrant tried to gather enough strength to state his case over again with greater force, but the physical reactions to his near-drowning were becoming more insistent and he knew he would have to lie down or risk keeling over. The futility of attempting to do anything more to help Somerville, Myrah and the others bore down on him like a massive weight. He stared dumbly at Martine for a moment, then turned and left the laboratory on legs which buckled gently with every step.

The small room in which he was installed contained a single bunk, a wardrobe, and a table and chair. There was a date, course and speed displayed on one wall—denoting that the accommodation was of officer standard—and in the outer wall there was a fixed porthole. When he was alone Tarrant went to the porthole and stood looking out. The Pacific stretched away to the horizon, vast, empty and uncaring. Feeling utterly defeated, he went to the bunk and lay down. He began to wonder what sort of person Myrah had been in her previous existence, but exhaustion claimed him almost at once, dragging him down into unconsciousness.

*　　*　　*

Tarrant was summoned back to life by an insistent grip on his shoulder. He opened his eyes and gazed at the blistered metal ceiling. Just when it seemed identity and memory would forever elude him, he focussed on the bespectacled, watchful face of Theo Martine.

Reorientation was both immediate and unwelcome. He looked around the room, saw that the direction of the light had changed very little while he had been asleep, and at once was filled with resentment at having been recalled so soon to a world of responsibilities and insoluble problems.

"I'm awake," he grumbled, pushing Martine's hand away. "What do you want?"

"It's not what I want," Martine said. "It's what *you* want."

"All I want is some sleep."

"And what about your friend Somerville?"

"What?" Now fully awake, Tarrant raised himself on his elbows and saw that Martine was holding a radio message slip. "What's been going on?"

"Quite a lot," Martine said, his jovial persona again in evidence. "Several computers have been holding a conversation about you."

"So?" Tarrant stared blankly into the other man's face.

"When you told me about your flying career you didn't mention that you had received astronaut training."

"Astronaut! We called it kamikaze training. That's why I...." Tarrant sat upright, his nerves taut with apprehension. "What's this all about?"

"It's about saving your friends," Martine replied. "There's a way we might be able to do it—provided you're willing to fly a spaceship."

# CHAPTER THIRTEEN

The helicopter which picked up Tarrant and Martine was a high-speed machine with rotor-tip jets and the initials of the Marine Technology Board in bold lettering on its fuselage.

As soon as both men had been safely winched inside, it dipped its nose and accelerated away to the south-west with a surge of power which Tarrant found exhilarating. It was the first time in three years that he had been airborne and his whole body took part in remembering the sensations of flight. The experience would have been entirely pleasant had it not served as a reminder that—incredibly—he was soon to be reintroduced to another type of flying.

It was too noisy for normal conversation in the helicopter's passenger compartment, so he sat close to a window and stared down at the vivid blue ocean and its white-chevroned ships. The world's supply of petroleum was virtually exhausted, which meant that the small number of remaining aircraft were destined to grow even fewer, and men had flocked back to the highways of the sea. The generous physics of water buoyancy made the solar-cell-battery-motor combination viable as means of propulsion, and the ordinary traveller had once more learned to measure his journeys in weeks rather than hours. As a military aviator Tarrant had to some extent been insulated from the forces of technological necessity. Aloft again, he felt that the crews of the seemingly motionless vessels far below might have been members of an alien race. Certainly, they were a generation of new men with whom, at that moment, he felt very little in common.

Tired and dissociated, he slumped in his seat as the helicopter carried him towards an undisclosed destination. It stopped to refuel on a small and nameless atoll, then flew on to a larger island which was traversed by an airstrip. He and Martine were transferred to a fixed-wing aircraft which, after a two-hour flight, put down on yet another island which Tarrant suspected might be one of South Newzealand's acquisitions in the Kermadec group. They disembarked and were met by four civilians who greeted Martine warmly while appearing not to notice Tarrant's existence, and the group went towards an administration block at the edge of the airfield.

Tarrant, who was becoming used to his ambiguous role—somewhere between that of a prisoner and a valuable item of luggage—looked all around him as he walked. His attention was immediately caught by a large hangar whose blocky shape he recognised as having been specially designed to accommodate a Type 7 ion rider. He took a deep breath, finally convinced that it was all true, that he was committed to flying into interplanetary space in a century-old craft which had been none too reliable when it was new.

"Feeling okay?" Martine fell into step beside him.

"Of course," Tarrant said. "This is all routine for me."

Martine smiled sympathetically. "I'm sorry about all the cloak-and-dagger stuff. You'll be meeting Miss Orchard in a minute and she'll fill in the background for you—until then I'm not free to speak."

Tarrant had not heard Miss Orchard mentioned previously and his imagination conjured up an image of an archetypal stenographer, complete with high heels, short skirt and notebook. They entered the administration building, went up a flight of stairs, and passed through a series of interconnected offices where their four escorts discreetly faded from sight. Men and women working at desks and drafting machines glanced at them incuriously as they passed.

Finally Martine ushered Tarrant into a larger, square room which had a window overlooking the airfield and on the opposite wall—traditional appurtenance of the senior scientist and engineer—an old-style blackboard. A tall, plump,

143

scholarly-looking woman of about sixty was seated at an overflowing desk. She wore a loose-fitting grey dress and had her hair drawn back into a bun, but Tarrant's first impression of austerity was offset by the broad smile with which she greeted his appearance. Her teeth were strong and well preserved, but stained with tobacco.

"Miss Orchard," Martine said. "I'd like you to meet Hal Tarrant."

She nodded and flipped a pack of cigarettes at him. "Have a smoke, Hal—by the look of you, you're bloody near all-in."

Tarrant caught the pack and, although he had not wanted one, took out a cigarette to give himself time to adjust to Miss Orchard's manner, which was vastly different from that of the demure ladies of Cawley Island. He picked up a lighter from the desk and puffed the cigarette into life.

"Hasn't much to say for himself, has he?" Miss Orchard leaned back in her chair and surveyed Tarrant appraisingly.

"He's had a rough time," Martine replied.

"Nonsense! There's nothing like a quick drown before breakfast to set you up for the day." Miss Orchard grimaced at her own lack of finesse and pointed to a chair. "Do you want to sit down, Hal?"

"I'm all right," he said stiffly, still unsure of his ground.

"Take a seat anyway—you make the place look untidy standing there. You too, Theo." While they were sitting down Miss Orchard lit a cigarette with practised movements, all the while continuing to stare frankly at Tarrant. "From what I hear, you're lucky to be alive, young man."

He nodded. "I think I am."

"That tissue you had in your lungs might have had something to do with your survival, you know—by overriding the normal panic response to drowning."

"How do you ...?" Tarrant looked in surprise from her to Martine.

"Oh, I had the biologist on the *Trilby* carry out some tests on it while you were on your way here." Miss Orchard narrowed her eyes behind a screen of smoke. "On what's left of it, I should say. Destroying half the specimen in acid was one hell of bloody waste, Theo."

"That was my idea," Tarrant said. "I wanted to destroy all of it."

Martine leaned forward with his head tilted. "What sort of test did you organise?"

"I had Norden put a laboratory animal in a container with a small piece of the tissue."

"Nice." Martine nodded his approval. "And what happened?"

Tarrant tried to ignore the crawling sensation in his spine as Miss Orchard described how a white rat had nosed the black jelly, apparently under the impression it was a foodstuff. The tissue had been seen to flow into its mouth, and from that moment the animal's behaviour patterns had been highly abnormal. It had refused to take part in maze-running tests, had stopped responding to stimuli, and when deliberately presented with a chance to escape from the laboratory had bolted towards the side of the ship in an attempt to reach the sea. The biologist had recaptured and killed it, and was currently sectioning the lungs to investigate the link-up with the rat's central nervous system.

"I'll be interested to hear what he finds," Miss Orchard concluded, turning back to Tarrant. "What's the matter with you, young man?"

"If you really want to know about that tissue," Tarrant said, "try the experiment I suggested to Mr Martine this morning. Try swallowing some of it yourself."

"So you *have* got something to say." Miss Orchard looked pleased. "Do you know, Hal, that I'm Project Leader on the dysteleonics investigation?"

"Nobody told me."

"Are you surprised?"

"No."

"I see." A malicious glint appeared in Miss Orchard's eyes. "You don't think I'm too young and pretty for the job?"

"All I'm thinking about is that a friend of mine is going to be killed."

"I'm sorry." She looked genuinely apologetic. "Well, here's the position. Until today the biggest leap forward we managed to achieve on the dysteleonics thing came two years ago when we discovered the water planetoids which Bergmann had postulated. On the strength of that I managed to appropriate a space craft, and I even got funds for an expedition which would have obtained water samples and looked for a matter transceiver."

"What went wrong?"

"We've got all kinds of enemies in the Government—some of them I don't even know about. They let me keep the ship, but all of a sudden the Air Force decided it couldn't release any qualified pilots for research work."

"I'm not a qualified astronaut," Tarrant said, feeling a touch of coolness on his brow. "I flew three training missions."

"Three or thirty—it makes no difference."

Tarrant's jaw sagged. "Are you serious?"

"I mean that an ion ship isn't like a first-generation space capsule. You don't measure your fuel reserves in seconds. Once you're up there you can fly around to your heart's content—practise as much as you want."

"It's all so simple." Tarrant wondered if he had made the sarcasm sufficiently obvious. "Why didn't you get somebody else to do it a couple of years ago? An out-of-work janitor, perhaps, or a...."

"Don't go huffy on me, Hal," Miss Orchard said impatiently. "I'm the one who's offering you a ship—and a volunteer crew, as well. Of course, I'd want my interests properly looked after when you were up there."

Tarrant felt a sensation akin to drowning, and he made a damping movement with both hands. "Miss Orchard—what are you talking about?"

"As far as I'm concerned, I'm talking about proving a scientific theory. As far as you're concerned, I'm talking about saving the lives of your friends."

146

"How?"

Miss Orchard looked at him reproachfully. "I should have thought that was obvious—you need to destroy the central mass of the creature you refer to as Ka."

"I. . . ." Tarrant had difficulty in speaking. "I didn't think anybody was going to believe me about that."

"Most people wouldn't," Martine put in. "But we've satisfied ourselves that the scrap of tissue we got out of your chest isn't an autonomous unit. There has to be the equivalent of a biological broadcasting station somewhere."

"But you accept the principle of telepathy?"

Martine glanced at Miss Orchard, and she nodded. "We believe that dysteleonics transmission and a number of mental phenomena—including so-called telepathy—are manifestations of the same thing," he said. "I'm prepared to bet that a good dysteleonics detector, if such a thing existed, would show a weak dysteleonics field surrounding that blob of jelly. Surrounding our brains too, for that matter."

Tarrant tried to weigh the implications of Martine's words, but Miss Orchard's earlier statement was in the process of exploding in his mind like a depth charge, sending up fountains of idea-shards. He looked at her in awe.

"Did you say we should destroy Ka?" He fought to keep his voice steady. "You want me to go up there and kill Ka?"

She shook her head. "Let's try to be a bit more precise, Hal. I want that planetoid investigated at first hand—*you* want your friends released from an outside control which is endangering their lives." She paused to light another cigarette from the end of her first. "As a scientist, I would prefer the creature to be kept alive for study by my colleagues. Luckily, though, it won't be necessary for you to annihilate it completely—breaking up the central mass and reducing its connectivity should be enough for your purposes. As soon as its cohesion is gone the boosters in your friends' lungs will cease to be boosters, and they'll be themselves again.

"We'll have to work out a technique for expelling the tissue, of course. We could always half-drown them, but I think that method has a certain lack of elegance, don't you? Luckily we have...."

"Luckily, you say?" Tarrant gave a shaky laugh as he strove to rise up through the spate of words. "You've got nothing to lose."

"On the contrary, Hal," Martine said soberly. "Miss Orchard is risking her job and a long term in prison. By bringing you here instead of handing you over to the Navy we've made ourselves accessories to your nuclear bomb theft. By tomorrow morning we could all be under arrest."

The telephone on the desk blinked an amber light and Miss Orchard picked it up. She listened for a moment, set the instrument down and stubbed out her cigarette amid the ruins of others.

"Balls to tomorrow morning," she said brusquely. "There's an Admiralty plane on the way right now. Make up your mind what you're going to do, Hal—if you're going you'll have to blast off in less than three hours."

# CHAPTER FOURTEEN

In the three years since he had last worn a space suit Tarrant had forgotten most of the discomfort and indignity. The breathing mixture it was supplying him smelt strongly of rubber, plastics and cleaning fluids—a choking combination which served as a constant reminder that he was totally at the mercy of his life support system.

There were disconcerting popping and scraping sounds each time he moved his left arm—suggesting that the pressure seals in the elbow were not properly adjusted—and, as always seemed to happen, he had difficulty in connecting his relief tube to the ship's waste disposal system. In common with the other young pilots, he had often laughed at tales of the gruesome accidents which had befallen men who had been careless in that respect, but as he struggled to tighten slippery rings the old stories, apocryphal or not, no longer seemed funny. By the time he had made himself secure he was sweating profusely.

He sat back in the G-seat and looked over his shoulder at his four companions, all of whom were still fumbling in their laps. It struck him as ironic that the portion of a man's anatomy which was least amenable to the restraints of civilisation should also prove the most troublesome at a time like this, when he was about to prove that his technology was more than equal to the challenge of space.

"A sadist designed this thing," Martine growled, his breathing amplified by his microphone. "Probably a woman with a chronic case of penis envy."

"There's nothing to worry about—unless we suddenly lose pressure," Tarrant said. As he had expected, his words provoked a renewed flurry of elbow movements, and he smiled in enjoyment of his own touch of sadism. He turned back to make a last-second check on the flight instruments and controls. The Type 7 ship was a de-militarised version of the Type 6B on which he had done his basic training. Removal of the weapons consoles and associated equipment had made it possible to accommodate two extra seats on the flight deck. The resultant gaps in the interior trim had been blanked off with unpainted alloy sheeting, but the work had been neatly executed and the general appearance of the ship left Tarrant reasonably confident about his own safety. He depressed several buttons, caused data about the drive unit to be projected on to the windscreen in front of him, and was examining it when he noticed a cluster of lights moving above the eastern horizon.

"Aircraft on finals," he announced. "Must be our visitors."

"That's correct," came Miss Orchard's voice from the small tower. "Can you get off all right?"

"As long as they don't try to land down wind." Until that moment Tarrant had been sustaining himself on coffee and pep pills, but his tiredness and apprehension abruptly left him as he reached for the single thrust control lever. The feeling was similar to the one he had got in the early days at the beginning of an interceptor sortie, except that it was magnified and enhanced by the knowledge that when he reached the limits of the stratosphere his flight would have only just begun.

Spaceflight had never really been more than a dream, but it was a dream which had exerted such a powerful influence on men's minds that they had gone on pursuing it—for a time—even when it had become apparent that the Solar System had nothing more to offer, and that the stars were too far away. This, too, was the ultimate form of the dream—uncluttered by any need for skyscraper tanks of liquid explosive or armies of ground controllers. A man, alone if need be, could step into a craft smaller than Columbus's *Santa Maria*, and sail it, if he dared, beyond the atmosphere, beyond the Moon, and across the tides of space. The dream had faded because there was no fitting destination for such travellers, but on this occasion Tarrant had a goal and a purpose, and he could almost see himself as the protagonist in one of his childhood fantasies, riding skywards on a bright plume of fire.

He moved the thrust control lever forward and at once the distant sheds on each side of the airstrip were illuminated by a flare of light from the ship's exhaust cone. The ship moved along the runway, still heavy, being rocked and jolted by irregularities in the concrete surface. Tarrant advanced the lever in its slot and the twilight outside abated as the pink brilliance, caused by ions recombining in the exhaust, neared its maximum intensity. The runway streamed by, seemingly smoother now that the ship's wings were creating lift, and the marker lights on each side became continuous wavering glows. Tarrant held the pointed nose down until he had a comfortable margin of air speed, then eased back on the control stick. At once, effortlessly, the ship was airborne and there was nothing visible ahead but a rectangle of sky, sparsely patterned by major stars.

This was the moment, well remembered from his training flights, which offered the headiest satisfaction. He allowed himself to be driven back into the heavily padded seat as the ship burned its way up the invisible slopes of infinity. Unlike the position with first-generation space craft, there was no need to reach an escape velocity—the continuity of thrust available from the ion drive would have made it possible to go into space at walking speed, provided one did not mind the immense waste of energy. But Tarrant, who was in a hurry and also anxious to avoid running the century-old engine at peak output for longer than necessary, chose to get away from the Earth's greedy embrace in a short time.

By holding the acceleration steady at just over one gravity, he had taken them to the upper edge of the stratosphere in five minutes, and a further five minutes saw the ship spiralling out of the historic orbital levels. The Earth swam away beneath them, a blue immensity whorled with white. As the silence of space descended over the craft, Tarrant—who had been using the skills of an aircraft pilot until then—began refreshing his memory of space flying technique by testing the primary attitude control jets. He was relieved to find they were in a functional condition.

"So this is what it's like," Martine said, breaking his silence for the first time. "In a way it's almost nothing."

Tarrant looked back at him. "You want to take over?"

"I didn't mean that. It's just that there was so little ... fuss."

Tarrant nodded without speaking. People thought of 20th century space exploration with nostalgia because it provided the last perfect example of the Big Project. There was a romance about the long-lost ability to funnel billions of dollars and the energies of tens of thousands of men into the achieving of a single objective—especially a technological objective—and it still coloured racial thinking. Almost unnoticed, against a background of global trauma, the ion drive had been developed and made practical and then abandoned, but not before it had wrought a vast change in the realities of space flight. It had become possible for an individual to climb into a small ship and fly to, say, Venus simply by pointing the nose of the craft at the evening star and keeping going until he caught up with it.

Such a procedure would have been highly inefficient, but a brief session with a slide rule or hand-held calculator would have been sufficient to compensate for planetary movements and produce a reasonably effective flight plan. The same amount of work, coupled with some basic astrogation, made it just as easy to fly to an unseen objective like an asteroid. A final discrepancy of a million kilometres or of a few hours in the rendezvous time—disastrous to a 20th century chemically-driven craft—meant nothing more than an extra set of *ad hoc* course corrections.

In keeping with the premise that any experienced aircraft pilot could fly a space ship, Tarrant's astronaut training had been almost totally concerned with learning how to destroy satellites before their automatic defences destroyed him, but he was humanly reluctant to make this clear to Martine and the others.

"There's no need for any fuss," he said, "as long as everybody knows what they're doing."

He checked that the pressure shell had not begun to leak and that the air regeneration system was functioning, then told Martine and the three volunteers to open their helmets and conserve the oxygen supplies in their suits. Two of the young men—Gerald Osaka and Bram Scotland—were dysteleonics researchers, and the third was a marine biologist called Evan Petersdorff. Their preparation for the flight had consisted of some hours of theoretical instruction almost two years earlier, and their nervousness was evident from the way in which they grinned too easily when they met his eye, and began nodding agreement before he had reached the end of a sentence. They gave the impression of being resourceful and competent, however, and he was satisfied they were level-headed enough to be told the basic facts of life in space.

"As you already know," he said, "we're going to rendezvous with a planetoid made of sea water. It's the one on this side of the Solar System, which is why I'm interested in it, so we'll be there in a few hours. When we get there I'm going to park the ship about two kilometres out, and we will complete the journey on suit power only.

"If the planetoid is rotating—and we have good reason to believe it is—we will penetrate the surface near one of the poles. We have these suits which were specially modified, and no doubt tested, by Miss Orchard," Tarrant paused while the three youngsters gave their ready smiles, "so getting about inside the planetoid should be very easy, even for a non-swimmer. I've had a fair amount of experience with this type of suit, and I think I can promise you they won't give any trouble.

"You four will remain near the surface, collecting samples, taking readings, and doing whatever you have to do. I have my own work to take care of, but I'll be near you at all times and I foresee no difficulty at all in our wrapping the job up in two or three hours and getting back to the ship. After that, it's an easy ride home."

"Who's got the picnic hamper?" Scotland said.

Tarrant was careful to join in the laughter which ensued. "The principal element of risk—and I must tell you this—comes from the ion drive unit of this ship."

"It seems to be working very well," Martine commented in a calm voice.

"It's working perfectly, but I want everybody to be in possession of all the facts—just in case." Tarrant twisted in his seat so that he could face his audience. "I might as well tell you that I quit the Air Force three years ago because they were making me fly these things, and I didn't want to do it."

"What was your objection?"

"Let me put it this way—the South Newzealand Air Force designation for this ship is Type 7, but its original Brazilian designation was Interceptor Type 83 Mark R2. In case you're not familiar with the mark number system, the further through the alphabet you get the closer you are to flying a thing which is made of nothing but patches and plasticine. The term Interceptor means that the drive was originally rated for six hours at continuous maximum thrust—and that was a hundred years ago."

Petersdorff looked thoughtful. "But the Air Force must have overhauled the propulsion unit in the meantime."

"They tried that, but the units they tampered with always gave more trouble than the ones they left alone, so now they don't bother. The pile, alternators and ion guns come in a sealed pack and they leave them that way."

"Oh, Christ," Petersdorff breathed. "Did you have to tell us that?"

"Yes, but don't worry too much," Tarrant said. "I wouldn't have taken the ship up if I thought anything was going to go wrong with it, but I want everybody to stay strapped in their seats and only move around when absolutely necessary. Above all, if there's a loss of thrust don't allow yourselves to float—because it could come on again, without warning, at full boost and you might fall on something sharp. Even worse, you might fall on something delicate which we need."

As Tarrant went on to outline the safety procedures he had learned from more experienced pilots, he found his thoughts straying to a small boat which was slicing through the Pacific night, provided it had not already been located and turned into incandescent gas. The only reason Will Somerville was caught in such a deadly trap was that he had taken a friendly interest in another man's well-being. Tarrant had a yearning to set him free which went far beyond the obligations of his own code of ethics, but at the same time he found himself wondering about the girl called Myrah.

Her real personality was a mystery to him, and it would have been ridiculous to suppose they could have anything in common, yet she had a quality which in his mind distinguished her from the other two women. He could see the pallid nakedness of her everywhere he looked, and yet—perhaps for the first time in his life as an adult—he was overwhelmingly aware of an attractive female as a thinking individual, distinct and separate from all those physical attributes to which he was conditioned to respond.

It occurred to him that he might never have given Beth Kircher anything like a fair deal, and he was beginning to explore the novel idea when there was a slight fall-off in thrust from the ship's drive. He glanced at the control panels, verified the change in impulsion and was composing words of reassurance when he saw that none of his companions had noticed the minute loss of weight. Deciding there would be little point in making his amateur crew more edgy than they already were, he suggested they should try to sleep while he refined the flight calculations. He ran the revised performance parameter through the ship's minicomputer and established a new time for going into the deceleration phase which would span the second half of the journey.

During the next four hours there were three more marginal losses of thrust, and each time he computed a new flight profile on the assumption there would be no further deterioration. His instructors had told him that some drive units were inclined to be skittish in the early stages of operation, but the continued stepping down of output caused Tarrant some concern. He experimented with the various simplified controls, wishing he knew more about what lay beneath their housings, and then—playing a hunch—pulled the thrust control lever back a short distance and pushed it forward again to its original setting. There was an immediate boost in power, which caused someone behind him to give a low exclamation, and a glance at the instrumentation showed Tarrant the ship was back on the original acceleration of 1.1 gravities.

He stared at the thrust lever, appalled by what he might have discovered. The idea of controlling a ship on its progress through space was reduced to a preposterous fantasy unless the pilot could be certain of a number of basic engineering verities. High on the list, possibly at the top, was the requirement for a control linkage whose output had a perfect, fixed and unvarying relationship to the input. The guarantees a pilot demanded were routinely given by competent mechanical engineers, but—and this was every flier's nightmare—they could be invalidated by an incident as trivial as a fitter dropping a lighted cigarette into his overalls and consequently forgetting to insert a locking pin in a push-rod joint.

Tarrant had no way of knowing if he was dealing with something as criminally simple as that, or if the fault lay in the exotic equipment at the heart of the drive unit, but suddenly he felt as though he was sitting on a time bomb. In particular, he disliked the possibility that the engine might cease delivering thrust altogether, especially at the peak velocities of turn-around time, in which case the ship was destined to carry five skeletons on a sight-seeing tour of the galaxy.

The sight of the Earth-Moon system shrinking to a brilliant double star failed to distract Tarrant's mind from his fears. He maintained a broody silence until it was time to shut down the drive and reverse the direction of thrust, then he carried out the manoeuvre with painstaking deliberation, his senses alert for the slightest discrepancy between what the ship was doing and what he was commanding it to do.

There was no trouble at any point in the procedure, and with the engine configuration changed to bring the forward ion guns into play, he gradually advanced the thrust lever in its slot. His morbidly sensitive touch could detect no sloppiness or lack of response as the increasing thrust pushed him forward against his seat harness.

Somewhat mollified, Tarrant turned his seat to the aft-facing position and forced himself to relax. He was now positioned behind the rest of the crew, looking over the backs of their seats and through the rear canopy of the flight deck. The ship's tail fins, illuminated by the drive flare and marker lights, were as steady as structures implanted in bedrock, and the slow wheeling of the stars beyond them was comfortingly like that caused by the Earth's diurnal rotation.

Tarrant thought again about Myrah, and in a few seconds was in the heavy, dreamless sleep of exhaustion.

The planetoid was a crescent of searing brilliance whose horns spanned the entire field of view from the forward canopy, and in the absence of spatial referents Tarrant had difficulty with orientation. As far as his senses were concerned he could have been a million miles out from an object the size of Jupiter. Only the obvious changes in the planetoid's aspect as he jockeyed the ship into position told him he was close to what, in cosmic terms, was a relatively insignificant body.

At a radar height of two kilometres above the northern pole he began work on the tricky task of matching velocities with the planetoid. The ship had not been provided with instrumentation suitable for measuring slow drifts, and Tarrant had to improvise as best he could with the coarse navigational equipment and direct sightings. It was only necessary to satisfy himself that, during a crew sortie of several hours, the ship would not blunder into the planetoid or recede beyond the effective range of the miniature propulsion units in the space suits, but a good twenty minutes of shunting and balancing had gone by before he felt any degree of confidence about quitting the ship.

"That's it," he announced finally. "We can go now."

The others had grown noticeably more tense during the prolonged and cautious manoeuvring, and to offset their mood he locked all the flight controls with a series of confident flourishes. The last one he touched was the thrust control lever. It travelled perhaps a centimetre along its slot before locking into the zero impulsion notch. Tarrant, who had been under the impression it was already in the last notch, felt his mouth go dry. He signalled the others to make ready to leave the ship and, trying not to be too obvious about it, he ran a final check on their position relative to the planetoid. Within the limits of observational error, it was unchanging. The only conclusion he could draw was that there had been a short period in which the control system had been demanding thrust and the drive unit had not been supplying it.

Martine floated into view beside him. "Something wrong, Hal?"

Tarrant hesitated, then decided to confide his alarm. "There seems to be a bit of free play in the thrust control linkage. When the lever position indicated the drive was on, it was actually off."

"It must have been in the lowest ranges."

"The very bottom."

Martine gave the equivalent of a shrug with his eyebrows. "I shouldn't worry about it."

"It's not your...." Tarrant hesitated. "All right—let's go."

While they were sealing their helmets and assembling the equipment for the expedition, Tarrant secretly pondered those traits in his character which had rendered him unsuitable for the profession of astronaut. Did he suffer from an excess of imagination? Or, was he—quite simply—a coward? To him it seemed blindingly obvious that a drive unit which was off when it should have been on could, with the lethal arbitrariness of a flawed machine, decide to be on when it was supposed to be off. The trouble was that his principal commitment of the hour was the shepherding of four inexperienced men on their first space walk, and to do it effectively he would have to inspire them with confidence in himself and in all the artifacts upon which their lives depended. He pushed the vague forebodings to the back of his mind and concentrated on the practicalities of preparing to destroy an enemy he had never seen, and which was protected by a cocoon of water many kilometres in thickness.

The torpedo which Miss Orchard's technicians had hastily cobbled together for Tarrant's use had started life as a deep-ocean, self-propelled camera sled. They had removed the photographic equipment and replaced it with fifty kilos of commercial explosive wired to detonate in proximity to a mass as large as they conceived the matter transceiver to be. The theory, explained by Miss Orchard with the aid of blackboard sketches, was that although the transceiver was drawing in water at a rate great enough to set up far-reaching currents there would be a dead spot—corresponding to the low-pressure zone behind a moving body—close to its inactive side.

"You'll appreciate that we're working on very low-grade evidence," Miss Orchard had said, "but, if we grant the existence of this monster of yours, that's where it has to be. I'm having a gravimeter fitted to the sled to enable it to find its own way to the centre of the planetoid, and when it gets to within five hundred metres or so the charge will detonate. At that range the shock wave won't damage the transceiver, but it should play hell with any organism as loosely constructed as a siphonophore."

She had paused to give Tarrant and Martine a malign

smile. "It would probably be enough for your purpose if you only succeeded in wafting the beast out of the dead spot and into the current. It would probably come apart quite nicely in that case."

The conversation had impressed Tarrant with the ability of the scientific mind to pursue a thread of logic to the end, regardless of the twists and turns on the way, and it kept returning to his mind while he made ready to leave the ship.

As soon as he had checked on his companions' suits Tarrant bled the flight deck air into space and opened the forward canopy. This operation was new to him and he was unprepared for the sense of awe which held him as the canopy parted like the wing-casings of an insect, putting him in direct communion with silent expanses beyond. He experienced in an intensified form a childhood feeling that the first step of a long journey was just as significant as the last, that the road itself was somehow mysterious and frightening because it extended from the familiar present to an unknown future.

As he was unstrapping the sled from its anchorages he was acutely aware—and the knowledge both chilled and exhilarated him—that were he to push a small object away from him, no matter how gently, it would begin a slow flight which might last for ever, and if he imparted spin to it the object would still be rotating at the same rate a million years later. Every movement he made seemed to have implications for eternity.

Trying not to let himself be distracted, Tarrant guided the sled out into the vacuum while the others were experimenting with their suit propulsers. The miniature thrusters were positioned on the lower edges of the backpacks, supposedly at each individual's centre of gravity, but there was an unavoidable degree of eccentricity and it took some practice before a man could progress through space without gently tumbling head over heels. Finally, however, the five were gathered around the sled with all their equipment, and began their descent to the planetoid. They remained silent as the globe of water expanded to meet them.

The layer of mist which covered the sunward side appeared to be quite thin and Tarrant soon was able to distinguish a greenish mottling here and there. This, he deduced, was caused by the vegetation which thrived in the freakish conditions and among whose deep-probing roots Myrah's people still lived.

Pressure of events had prevented him from thinking much about that strange offshoot of the human race—a lost tribe of two hundred men, women and children—but they represented a problem which he and others would soon have to face. The grand plan laid down by Bergmann's ancient technocrats made no provision for them, and they were doomed to extinction as their world shrank to nothing, unless a major effort could be made to bring them back to Earth. There were enough serviceable space craft littered around the planet to form a rescue fleet, but international co-operation on that scale was no longer feasible. A remote possibility was that they might be contacted and persuaded to swim voluntarily into the maw of the matter transceiver, but the obstacles along that route were so numerous that Tarrant's mind shied away from considering them. His present burden of responsibility was already in danger of becoming insupportable. . . .

At a height of about one kilometre he gave the order to decelerate and began squirting jets of compressed gas from the suit's forward nozzle. As the surface of the planetoid drew nearer he saw that it was not as even as he had at first supposed. Hillocks of water arose and gradually subsided in response to internal forces, their peaks sometimes emerging through the covering mist, creating the impression that the entire globe was a living entity. The notion led Tarrant's thoughts in the direction of the dark, sentient core of the planetoid, and he felt a return of the unmanning revulsion and dread which had been inspired in him by the sight of a small fragment of Ka-tissue.

Miss Orchard had confidently stated that fifty kilos of

explosive would bring about the loss of connectivity necessary to reduce Ka to mindless protoplasm, but such assurances meant little when it came to a confrontation with the living enormity, the vast obscenity that was Ka. Tarrant became aware of the harsh, irregular sound of his own breathing, and knew it would be transmitted by the suit radio.

"Retain some velocity and go in feet first," he said, taking refuge in practicalities. "We can muster again just below the surface and start getting used to...." His voice was lost in a prolonged burst of static which lasted until the surface of the planetoid had been transformed into a vapour-shrouded plain only metres beneath him. Tarrant's bafflement lasted perhaps a second, then he looked back over his shoulder and saw a very small, intensely brilliant constellation in stealthy movement against the hinterland of fixed stars.

"No!" he shouted, rationality swept away. "You can't!"

There was a soft impact and suddenly he was in a clear blue universe where the suited figures of his companions threshed amid sprays of silver bubbles. He stabilised himself automatically and brought the sled under control at the end of its short tether. Other men clustered around him, making uncertain movements with their arms and legs, looking remarkably similar to divers in conventional underwater gear. The surface of the water, disturbed by their arrival, undulated nearby like a blanket of white fire.

"That radio interference," Bram Scotland said, "was it from the ship's ion guns?"

"We've lost her," Tarrant replied tersely.

"Lost her! What do you mean we've lost her?" Petersdorff closed with Tarrant, the panic-pitch of his voice slipping beyond his suit transducer's range. "What sort of a bloody pilot are you?"

Tarrant fended him off. "It looks as though the drive unit was only dormant."

"You bastard!" Petersdorff shouted. "I said, what sort of a bloody pilot are you supposed to be?"

"Your people had the ship for two years. That was long enough to make sure...."

"This is wasting time," Martine put in. "Hal, is there any chance of catching her? Using the suit thrusters?"

"No chance. No chance at all."

"Does that mean we're finished?" Gerald Osaka said, speaking for the first time.

Petersdorff turned to him, flailing a huge bubble out of his way. "What else can it mean?"

"I'll tell you what it means, gentlemen." Martine spoke in a calm but authoritative voice. "It means—and Hal will confirm this—that we go back to Earth the quick way. Through the matter transceiver."

# CHAPTER FIFTEEN

The strange little conference lasted fifteen minutes.

Tarrant knew that oxygen supplies were being expended—and, at another level of his consciousness, he was acutely aware that time was running out on Will Somerville and Myrah—but he was unable to countenance taking the group to the centre of the planetoid without explaining the dangers involved. Petersdorff, Osaka and Scotland had been told nothing of the events leading up to their first space flight. They listened to Tarrant's story with quiet concentration, acceptance encouraged by the desire to believe they could return to Earth, and by the bizarre circumstances in which the account was presented. Petersdorff, after his initial outburst, developed a manic cheerfulness which abated only slightly when he learned that he might have to face the malign creatures known as the Horra. It appeared that his professional interest in marine biology was overcoming his concern for his own safety. Osaka and Scotland, the dysteleonics men, had greater difficulty in comprehending all that was implied by the monosyllable, Ka.

"You believe this ... *thing* started off as a single medusa fish," Scotland said, "then incorporated other organisms into itself. It's hard to believe that such a...."

"The same thing on a smaller scale has been happening on Earth for millions of years," Petersdorff interrupted. "Your ordinary Portuguese man-of-war is actually a colony of hundreds of polyps, all of which...."

"The point is that we have to kill it," Tarrant said, raising his voice. "Kill it or disperse it—otherwise we may not reach the transceiver. Any more comments?"

Scotland raised an arm. "We'd better not waste any more time, Hal. If there are ten or twelve Bergmann machines scattered around the Earth, as we believe, the water is almost certain to be delivered to all of them in rotation."

"You mean...?" Tarrant looked at Martine for confirmation.

"It's a good point," Martine said. "We'd better just pray the transceiver is still delivering to the Cawley Island region—I couldn't take a thousand-kilometre swim."

The new uncertainty, the new variable in the problem, served to increase Tarrant's sense of urgency. "How far is it to the centre of this place? Ninety kilometres?"

"About that."

"Can we go that far on suit air? Even if we could swim at a steady five kilometres an hour it would take...."

"Swimming is out," Martine cut in. "We've only got enough breathing gas for about five hours, so we'll have to ride the sled most of the way down, and break free before your bomb goes off."

Without waiting for reactions to his words, he caught hold of the sled and manoeuvred himself into position at its control panel. Grateful for the positive leadership, Tarrant swung in beside him. As soon as the three other men had tethered themselves to the tubular framework, Martine activated the automatic control circuits and pressed the button which ignited the sled's engine. There was a dull, continuous roar from within the combustion chamber, the caged propeller began to spin, and the sled moved off at once with the serene purposefulness of a robot device. It hunted in slow circles for a few seconds, then its sensors determined the direction of the planetoid's faint gravity and its nose swung sharply downwards.

Tarrant discovered immediately that all his previous experience of supersonic flight through an invisible medium had been bland and monotonous compared to the roller-coaster dash through galaxies of solid-seeming bubbles which rushed to meet him and darted frantically to each side as they encountered the sled's bow wave. When he looked behind him he saw them shattered and transformed into millions of opals and pearls which stretched upwards towards the light in the form of intertwined spirals created by the propeller wash. To his astonishment, the speed shown on the sled's control panel was less than thirty kilometres an hour.

"We're only getting one shot at this, so let's not treat it as a joyride," Martine shouted above the flurry of turbulence. "Can you take water samples, Evan?"

"I'm doing it," Petersdorff replied, fumbling with the equipment on his belt. "Trying to avoid contamination from the exhaust."

Scotland and Osaka steadied themselves as best they could and began taking readings from an assortment of instruments on their wrists and chest panels, while Martine started shooting film with a miniature camera attached to his helmet. Excluded from the activity, temporarily relieved of all responsibility, Tarrant nestled into the sparse protection of the sled and watched the alien world stream past him. The ambient light began to fade, but at a very much slower rate than if they had been plummeting into one of the Earth's oceans. He wondered if this was solely because the planetoid was closer to the sun and unscreened by an atmosphere, or if it was a geometrical effect by which the globe of water served as a huge optical condenser.

Martine would doubtless have an answer, but the enquiry could wait until later. A torpor was settling over Tarrant as a result of the intense emotional and physical stress throughout a period which felt like years, although his memory could account for only three full days since his first encounter with the big squid. He closed his eyes and allowed his senses to be swamped by tiredness and the pervasive, choking odour of rubber, plastics and cleaning fluids circulating within his suit.

"Theo! Are the bomb circuits active?" Scotland's voice reached him a short time later, and he forced his eyes open.

"Of course not," Martine answered.

"That's good—I've got indications of a large metal object

166

about ten kilometres away from us. Over that way."

"Do you think it's the ...?"

"Not a chance. This object isn't very massive. In fact, there might be more than one."

"I'd like to take a look at it," Tarrant said, now fully alert, intuitions stirring.

"So would I, though we haven't much time." Martine made an adjustment on the sled's control panel and signalled for Scotland to join him. The square steering vane ahead of Tarrant wavered uncertainly for an instant as Scotland assumed control, then the sled veered off its radial course. They were plunging through a blue twilight in which root forests appeared as distant vertical shadings of indigo. Tarrant peered out in front and within a few minutes began to distinguish a patch of darkness. The sled's propeller stopped turning and went into reverse, forcing him to alter his grip on the structure, and at the same moment somebody switched on the photographic floodlights in the nose of the sled. Tarrant's eyes widened reflexively as a fantastic scene sprang into view ahead of him.

The hull of a flying boat, minus the wings, glimmered in the rippling luminescence like the carcase of a giant whale. Its outlines were obscured by skeins of nets, and it was trailing a complex spawn of large inflated bags secured by webs of rope. Surrounding the central mass were the figures of more than a hundred men and women, attached to it by individual tethers and frozen by the sudden brilliance of the lamps in the act of towing it through the water. They were naked except for belts around their waists and hemispherical, flower-like cages strapped to their heads.

This, Tarrant knew at once, was the Clan of which Myrah, Lennar and the others had spoken. Until that moment these people had been an abstraction to him, and he found their multitudinous, living reality almost too much for his comprehension. The exclamations he could hear within his helmet told him the rest of his group were undergoing the same reaction. As he stared at the clustered swimmers he became aware that, although they had halted their progress through the water, they were not entirely at rest—at every second some of them were making odd darting movements of their heads as they captured slow-drifting air bubbles. Tarrant experienced a sympathetic constriction in his own chest as he imagined spending an entire lifetime in conditions where the simple act of breathing called for such unremitting activity. His respect and pity for the humans in the isolated little colony crystallised into a kind of anguish as he saw they were shielding their eyes and at the same time preparing to defend themselves with slim, spear-like weapons.

"Turn out the lights," he snapped. "We're frightening them."

The brilliance faded immediately and a long, pulsing minute went by while his eyes adapted to the lower level of illumination. Strange as the conglomeration before him was, Tarrant realised it did not correspond with the description of the Home given to him by Lennar.

The only conclusion he could reach was that the Home had been abandoned, probably because its flimsy structure was being disrupted by the current, and that the members of the Clan were migrating in search of still water. He guessed that within the flying boat hull were all those who could not survive for a long time in open water—the infants, the sick and the aged. The problem facing these heroic people, although they had no way of knowing it, was that their quest for a new resting place could only be successful in the short term. As the planetoid shrank over a period of years the currents would become stronger and further reaching, and the inevitable outcome would be total extinction of the Clan in any of a number of ways....

"More evidence to back your story, Hal," Martine said, almost reverently. "I guess we ought to try speaking to them."

Tarrant began detaching himself from the sled. "This is my job. Can you hold this position while I go closer?"

"Okay—but remember we're short of time. What are you going to say, anyway?"

"I...." Tarrant hesitated. "I have to persuade them to follow us down and go through the transceiver."

Martine snorted. "Good luck!"

"Thanks." Tarrant pushed himself away from the sled and began swimming towards the colony.

"Just one thing," Martine called after him. "My first responsibility is to my own men, so I can only give you ten minutes—and if they start throwing those spears we can't go after you."

"Understood."

Tarrant continued swimming, hampered by the space suit, until he was some ten metres from the nearest of the Clan. They watched his progress intently, faces partly veiled by reflections on the surfaces of trapped bubbles, weapons at the ready. He tried to go closer before speaking, but several of the spears were making tentative jabbing movements which told him their owners were on the very point of throwing.

"I am a friend," he said, enunciating as clearly as possible. "I want to talk to you."

The shock caused by his voice was apparent from the way in which the listeners went rigid for an instant, some of them drawing back while others tightened their grips on their spears. There was a confused babble of response, the sounds fracturing on air-water interfaces. Its general tone was obviously hostile.

"I am a friend," he repeated, then it occurred to him that to these people he had to resemble a creature from a nightmare. "I am a man, a human—just like you."

"You do not breathe," an older man shouted, brandishing his spear.

Tarrant spread his arms and legs to demonstrate his human shape, "I breathe. I have air in here." He tapped his helmet.

"Not enough air for a man."

Realising the futility of attempting to explain the functioning of his suit, Tarrant tried a different tack. "I am a friend of Lennar, and Myrah, and Geean, and Treece, and Harld."

There was another ripple of surprise, and a woman cried, "They're dead! It comes from Ka!"

"They are not dead," he said, trying to project reassurance across the gulf of incomprehension. "They are alive. I bring you news of them."

"Leave us, child of Ka."

Tarrant surveyed the scene helplessly, and tried to remember the name of the Clan leader which had been given to him. "I want to talk to ... Solman."

This time there was a different kind of response, one which gave the impression of being less hostile, and several white figures swam towards the deep-bodied shape of the flying boat hull. Tarrant trod water to hold his position, and waited in silence. A minute later an elderly man with white, wispy hair swam towards him with ungainly strokes. His joints were visibly swollen with arthritis, and he was flanked by younger men whose duty it was to shepherd air bubbles into the filigreed cage which surrounded his head like a halo. He advanced as far as the front rank of his people then halted, his face impassive.

"Are you Solman?" Tarrant said.

"I am Solman." The voice was hoarse, but firm and with an imperious quality to it. "How do you know my name?"

"Lennar told it to me."

"I sent Lennar to his death."

"Lennar is not dead. He is alive and...." Tarrant stopped short of saying that Lennar was well. "I have come here to help you. To bring you to Lennar and his friends."

"Where are they?"

Tarrant took a deep, quavering breath and launched into an attempt to describe, using the vocabulary of a child, the history of two worlds and two peoples, plus the theory of the Bergmann machines and their role in stabilising the land area of Earth. But long before he had begun to speak of a "gateway" at the centre of the globe of water, and of

170

Solman's duty to lead the people of the Clan through it, he saw the beginnings of the older man's smile—which was both compassionate and scornful—and he knew he was defeated. He fell silent.

"I am grateful to you, child of Ka," Solman said. "You have given me reassurance ... that Ka has grown feeble. So feeble that he has to plead for us to give our bodies up to him."

Tarrant stretched out his hands. "You don't understand."

"I understand all." Solman glanced at the men and women near him and they nodded gravely, reaffirming his mandate.

"But...." Tarrant thought of all the occasions in the past when he had found it impossible, even when speaking to a friend from his home town, to explain his ideas on clear-cut, familiar issues in words which retained the same meaning between leaving his lips and arriving at the other person's ears. He looked at Solman, at the arrays of naked bodies suspended at the ends of their lines in a dim continuum of blue shade and silver bubbles, at the brooding hulk of the wingless flying boat whose present owners would never understand its original purpose—and a new kind of pain was born inside him.

"Time's up, Hal." Martine's voice reached him across an immense distance. "We have to go."

"I have to go," Tarrant repeated like a compliant child.

Solman pointed downwards. "Return to your master."

Tarrant backed off a short distance by pushing at the water with his hands and feet, then turned and swam to the sled. In the blue half-light, even to his eyes, the four bulky, helmeted figures waiting by it could have been creatures worthy of the name, children of Ka. The sled itself looked like a squat marine creature, a diablo, with knowing, watchful eyes.

He returned to his niche behind the starboard fin and snap-hooked himself in place as the engine growled into life. Guided once again by its sensors, the sled began boring down towards the heart of the world, and as it picked up speed

Tarrant had a final glimpse of the people of the Clan.

Indomitable, pragmatic, they had already begun to swim towards a haven which existed nowhere but in their own dreams.

Commander Leon P. Cavray, of the South Newzealand Navy, stared thoughtfully at the tactical display projected on the main screen in his operations room. His own ship—the corvette *Dalton*—was represented near the bottom of the screen by a slim ellipse from which sprouted an arrow indicating course and speed. A number of other vessels were scattered over the ten thousand square kilometres of the South Pacific covered by the display, and were indicated by various symbols. The image intensities of all but one had been muted—the exception being a red triangle which pulsed with an angry brilliance.

"That's *The Rose of York*," said Naipur, the weapons officer. "There's no doubt about it."

Cavray fingered his short beard. "You think there's no doubt about it."

"Excuse me, sir, but that's a contradiction in terms."

"I know."

Naipur sighed noisily, not troubling to hide his impatience. He was a neat, ambitious man who had carried out a thousand successful long-range engagements of enemy ships on training simulators, and who desperately wanted to test himself and his charges in a real situation. The dispassionate peace which lay over the world, coupled with the growing scarcity of reliable Seafire nuclear torpedoes, had led him to despair of ever adding combat honours to his service record. And now that a perfect, heaven-sent chance had come his way he was baffled by his captain's reluctance to carry out Staff orders.

"It's in exactly the right area," he said. "It's exactly on course for Harpoon, it refuses to enter into radio communication, and all the other vessels in the designated area have been eliminated. What more do you want?"

"I'd like visual confirmation."

"To get that you'd have to go in close—and in a nuclear situation you can't do that." Naipur strode across the room and tapped the bright-flaring symbol with his finger. "This is *The Rose of York*."

Cavray looked mildly surprised. "That, Mr Naipur, is a red triangle on a map. Send out a reconnaissance drone."

"We've only got one left, and it'll take a good thirty minutes to check it out."

"All combat equipment is supposed to be in a state of instant readiness," Cavray reproved. "But if you get the drone airborne within fifteen minutes I won't mention this lapse in my report."

"Thank you, sir." Naipur gave a very correct salute, his face expressionless, and walked to the door. As soon as he was in the narrow gangway outside the operations room he broke into a silent-footed run, heedless of the stares of the ratings he almost collided with on his way to the weapons hangar.

As the darkness began to grow more intense around the sled Martine switched on its forward lights. Their twin beams lanced straight ahead, creating the illusion that the sled was winging along an alley swarming with alien life. Air bubbles appeared as solid globes of mercury which rushed forward, threatening in their massiveness, only to disperse harmlessly in the invisible bow wave. A dozen varieties of fish darted into the surrounding gloom or formated with the sled, effortlessly keeping pace with its descent.

"The lights aren't a good idea," Tarrant said. "They're making us too conspicuous."

"Okay. If you...."

"Leave them on a minute," Petersdorff said. "I can use some film of the fish."

"Film?" Tarrant raised his voice in exasperation. "A few hours ago you were...."

He broke off as—with frightening suddenness—the nightmarish shape of a big squid appeared out of the murk, swimming parallel with the sled. The great triangular fins along the side of the pointed fore-body writhed in a succession of sine waves, the tentacles pulsed in time with the creature's breathing, and a huge eye reproached the five men for having strayed beyond their natural bounds. Tarrant's mouth twisted in shock as he saw other similar outlines materialising from the darkness. He reached for the only underwater weapon he possessed, which was a sheath knife.

"Something else you were right about, Hal," Petersdorff shouted, sounding almost happy. "Definitely a giant form of *Loligo vulgaris*."

Tarrant tried to squeeze further into his niche. "For God's sake watch out!"

"It's all right—they won't attack anything as big as the sled."

One of the squid swooped in close to the starboard side of the sled, coming to within an arm's length, and Tarrant— past caring what others might think of him—reacted by giving a full-throated scream. He struck out with the knife, but the squid moved effortlessly beyond his reach, then closed again.

"Take it easy, Hal." Petersdorff's voice registered surprise and concern. "They're just curious."

"I don't like the brutes, either," Martine said. "What can we do to get rid of them?"

"Try the lateral photofloods."

A second later there was a searing flash of brilliance from each side of the sled, and the squid vanished before it like phantoms. Tarrant gave a sob of relief and tried to steady his breathing as the lights were doused. He could hear Martine and Petersdorff having a whispered argument above him, and guessed Martine was pointing out how much he had gone through in the previous three days. Tarrant knew he should be grateful, but all at once he felt no more obligation to be courageous or disciplined. For what seemed an eternity he had been frightened, shocked, threatened, violated,

174

punished—and now he was reaching the limit of what he could take. Life had become a nightmare in which somebody had thrown away all the old rulebooks, and he felt entitled to do the same. With luck he would be back on Earth within another hour or so, and if that happened he was going to live exactly as he pleased from then on, and in the meantime he was going to hang back and let others take the responsibilities and the risks, and if anything scared him he was going to let the whole universe know he was scared, and if he had to die he was going to claim the right to go out kicking and cursing and screaming.

Curled up in as small a compass as he could attain with the bulk of the suit, Tarrant clung to the framework of metal struts and watched the darkness gather around as the sled continued on its reckless plunge into the centre of the planetoid. He ignored all attempts to draw him into communication. After a time the others accepted his new passive role, and he realised this with a flicker of pleasure. The appearance of the Horra was not repeated, but it was no longer possible for him to drift off into semi-consciousness. In spite of his exhaustion, he remained alert and nervous, and all the while the darkness became more complete....

"I don't see how this can be," Theo Martine was saying, many light years away. "We're bound to be within ten kilometres of the centre."

"I know," Scotland replied. "That's what's bothering me."

"You're sure your instruments are working?"

"Positive."

"I confirm the readings," Osaka said. "There aren't any sizeable chunks of metal or anything else up ahead of us."

There was a lengthy pause before Martine spoke again. "That leaves us with two possibilities, gentlemen—the transceiver is built of some substance which doesn't register on our instruments; or ... *or* the system doesn't require the physical presence of a machine at the target location."

Tarrant listened to the words from his remote cocoon of loneliness, and—without his quite knowing why—a mood of bitter sadness began to steal over him.

"It might explain why there are two planetoids," Osaka said. "If there's no physical transceiver, the water must have been transmitted to a target location at the united focus of the Bergmann machines on Earth—but the sun must have got in the way every now and then. It would have been logical to switch to an alternative target location."

"I like it," Martine said. "I like that a lot."

Tarrant's sadness increased, causing him to squeeze his eyes shut, contorting his whole face in protest. He waited, straining his ears for words which had yet to be spoken.

"Of course," Martine continued, "it means that the Special Products team have balled up the design of this bomb we're riding around on. The proximity fuse won't function unless there's something for it to be proximate to."

"Any chance of modifying it? Putting in a timer?"

"Underwater? In the dark? With no tools or components?"

"This is all to the good," Scotland said. "Instead of letting the sled go ahead by itself ... leaving us to swim God knows how far in the dark ... we can switch on all the lights and go down-current at full speed ... right through the gate. The sled has buoyancy bags, hasn't it? We'll even have transportation when we come out on the other side."

Tarrant fought a battle against his own psychic inertia. "We're not going to do it that way."

"It's come to life again," Petersdoff whispered incredulously. "It spoke!"

"This sled is my responsibility," Tarrant said.

"Just like the ship was."

"That's enough, Evan." Martine's voice cut sharply through the blackness and the blur of other sounds.

Petersdorff was not subdued. "We had a ship to take us back to Earth. And we lost the ship. So now we go back on the sled."

"Nobody is disputing that," Martine said angrily.

"I am," Tarrant countered, straightening up against the onrushing flow of water so that he could be closer to Martine.

"Hal, I know how you feel." Martine touched his shoulder briefly. 'Believe me, I know what's going on in your mind—but here are the facts. The simple, engineering facts."

He went on to give a detailed description of the electrical system which had been put together in such haste to detonate the sled's explosive charge. His words, emotionless and academic, carried all the more conviction for the grotesque circumstances in which they were being delivered. And in spite of Tarrant's mental turmoil, he eventually had to accept that it was impossible—because of the underwater environment—even to carry out a suicide mission in which the bomb would have been triggered manually.

"It isn't anybody's fault," Martine concluded, trying to offer the absolution Tarrant needed. "The system just isn't adaptable."

"We're starting to pull across current," Bram Scotland said, the outline of his helmet faintly visible in the glow from the sled's control panel. "We must be nearly there."

Martine turned away from Tarrant at once. "Take her off automatic. Go with the current."

"Do you want the big lights?"

"Not yet—save them in case we run into trouble."

Tarrant stared ahead, into the dark heart of the world, and an arctic coldness developed in his gut as he thought about Martine's final words to him. Every organism, every mechanism, was conditioned by its environment—and, if the environment changed, failure to adapt meant failure to function and survive. This applied to electrical circuits, dinosaurs, civilisations. As he became aware of the awful conclusion which was surfacing through resistant layers of his mind, Tarrant tried to stop thinking altogether, but the logical processes—having been set in ponderous motion—could not be halted.

Man was supreme on Earth, even in this latter day, because he had been given many opportunities to be flexible, and had taken them. Man was doomed to extinction in this alien globe because he had lost most of his adaptive capability.

*Not enough air for a man*, the nameless member of the Clan had said, unable to enlarge his world-view to accommodate a new reality.

*Return to your master*, Solman had said, unable to think in new categories.

*Fifty kilos of high explosive*, Miss Orchard had said, arriving at an old solution to a new problem.

As he felt the sled change course to go with the current, Tarrant—knowing that the others were too preoccupied to be aware of his actions—opened the snap-hook which held him secure. He kicked himself free of the sled, and within a few seconds was completely alone in the black waters which were the stronghold of an enemy he would never see.

Commander Leon P. Cavray ground out a cigarette in a cluttered ashtray, while his eyes took in every detail of the picture on the television screen before him. The reconnaissance drone he had dispatched was little more than a ducted fan engine fitted with a camera pod, and therefore it could fly close to enemy craft with little risk of being seen or destroyed.

In this instance it was hovering a few hundred metres to one side of a cabin cruiser which was holding a steady northeast course on the prehistoric blue surface of the South Pacific. The clarity of the transmitted picture was exceptionally good, and Cavray could discern the name, *The Rose of York*, painted on the bows. He could also see the figure of a middle-aged man on the cruiser's bridge, a man whose name he knew to be Willard Somerville. The man was wearing a white shirt and a scrap of red material on his head, and he was looking neither to one side nor the other as his boat traced an invisible line towards Harpoon Island.

"Nice picture," Lieutenant Naipur said conversationally. "Nice. Clear."

Cavray eyed him coldly. "What's the precise range?"

"Eighty-seven kilometres, sir."

"Torpedo transit time?"

"Sixty-one minutes, sir. Plus one minute or minus three-point-five depending on current."

Cavray looked back at the screen and made one last attempt to understand why an obscure and law-abiding farmer should decide to throw his past life to the winds and become an international criminal. There had to be some explanation—and yet his knowing it would have changed nothing. His orders were clear, precise and immutable.

"All right, Lieutenant," he said tiredly. "Cast the first stone."

Naipur's face remained impassive. "Sir, is that an order to destroy the nominated vessel with a medium-range nuclear torpedo?"

"That's what it is. But in the meantime keep trying for radio contact."

"Very good, sir." Naipur turned to the waiting weapons controllers and gave a series of orders, and within twenty seconds a long, black cylinder—expelled from the mother ship in a plume of compressed air—was acquainting itself with the medium in which it had been designed to operate. It aligned its various axes in accordance with programmed instructions, selected its optimum cruising depth, and began boring through the water towards the position its quarry would occupy sixty-one minutes in the future.

The luminous dial on Tarrant's chest panel told him he had less than one hour remaining in his life support system, and hence he was grateful when the Ka-Horra took him.

His eyes being less well adapted to the darkness than those of Myrah or Lennar, he saw nothing of his captor or its fellows. He felt the sudden constriction of its tentacles around his body, and he heard the complex turbulence of its wake as it carried him down towards his rendezvous with Ka—but no images assailed his mind.

Tarrant was glad of this circumstance, because he had learned that his eyes were the pathways of fear. Sightless, and therefore immune, he was able to force himself to remain at rest until the ghastly flight had ended, and he knew he had been delivered into the jealous custody of his former master.

The unseen tentacles relaxed and floated away from him, and their hold was replaced by a more subtle constraint. A gentle, coaxing, all-enveloping pressure surrounded his body. He knew that black labia were drawing him inwards, that black pseudopods were probing and caressing him, that black membranes were curling and converging around him in dreadful simulation of the placental trophoblast which had once given him life.

He waited, unmoving, for perhaps a minute, sensing the inarticulate bafflement which must have been growing in the corded, living jelly, trying to judge the moment at which ingestion would turn to rejection. Eventually, unable to wait any longer, he reached for his knife. There was some resistance to the movement of his arm, but no more than if he had been forcing it through a deep pool of spawn.

*"You made a mistake, Ka,"* he chanted aloud—as he began to cut—and the words were punctuated by his gasps of exertion.

"In all your centuries of life ... *ah!* ... every being you encountered ... *ah!* ... man or squid or fish ... *ah!* ... shared the common need to breathe ... *ah!* ... and this has left you ... *ah!* ... with no flexibility of response ... *ah!* ... *ah!* ... *AH!"*

The hour which followed never subsequently became clear in Tarrant's memory.

It was a time of fever and of delirium, a time in which—to preserve his sanity—he delivered lectures and sermons on the necessity of being adaptable; on the need for absolute reliability in control systems; on the design of the simple space suit, the basic piece of engineering which enabled a man to exist in one world while breathing the air of another, and which for that reason meant life for him and death for Ka.

There were periods when the labour was comparatively easy, when he could sever tissues without the aid of the knife simply by flailing his arms and legs. There were other periods unbearably hideous in retrospect, when only the blade would do and he had to hack through organic ropes, billowing membranes, spongy clumps and clusters; or when he blundered against what felt like skeletal remains which moved in time with the convulsions of the surrounding tissue as though the original life force was imprisoned within them.

*Break up the central mass*, Miss Orchard kept saying, and laughing her raucous laugh. *All you have to do is reduce its connectivity....*

Finally, there came the moment when a crushing pain in his chest told him—or the part of his identity which was preserved in the eye of the storm—that his supply of breathing gas was almost exhausted, that his time of invincibility was drawing to a close. Knowing he had done all that could be asked of him, he headed for clear water, half-crawling and half-swimming, guided by blind instinct and desperation.

Several times on the journey he touched powerful, rubbery bodies and knew he had encountered the big squid—but now they were nothing more than that, and nothing less. No longer Ka-Horra, medusa's children, they were feeding eagerly on the abundant plasm which drifted all around them, extracting their own form of revenge on the being which had subverted their destinies.

The roar of the current, when it came, was louder to Tarrant than the pounding in his temples. He felt himself being thrown about at an ever-increasing pace, twisting and tumbling in a black maelstrom. The clamour of the waters grew louder, grew unbearable ... then there was light.

Tarrant struck out with the fleeting dregs of his strength, instantly aware that the space suit which had been so essential to the continuance of his life now represented a deadly threat because of its lack of buoyancy. He reached the surface, and was trying to open the helmet with one hand while swimming with the other, when he heard shouts in the distance. He fought to remain afloat, to fill his lungs with clean blue light, then he was gripped by strong hands and felt the angular solidity of the sled beneath him. Somebody opened his helmet, permitting him to gorge himself on the soft, fresh air of an October morning.

"We've been trying to keep this thing from sinking for the best part of an hour," Theo Martine grumbled. "Where have you been?"

# CHAPTER SIXTEEN

Tarrant and Somerville walked in silence to the single landing stage which had been erected in a small bay at the north end of Shad Island. The summer was well advanced and the plentiful vegetation above the high water line was gleaming with a peculiar intensity, as though the leaves had been freshly enamelled. Somerville's boat was riding peacefully at anchor, its solar panels drinking in energy for the voyage ahead.

"Are you sure you won't change your mind?" Tarrant said "There's a lot of work to be done here."

Somerville shook his head. "Not my kind of work. I'm a farmer, and that's all I ever want to be."

"Cawley Island is going to seem a bit tame, isn't it?"

"Not to me, young Hal." Somerville adjusted his red bandana to the correct slant across his forehead. "Do you know how far that torpedo was from me when I came to my senses and answered my radio?"

"I should do—you've told me about fifty times."

"Five kilometres! And probably a lot less by the time the destruct mechanism worked."

"That's all in the past." Tarrant shaded his eyes from the sun and looked at the low prefabricated building housing the shallow pools which were the nucleus of what Miss Orchard had dubbed the Aquarian Rehabilitation Centre. "We could use your help, Will."

"It isn't my line of business, I tell you."

"It isn't anybody's line of business—it's brand new to all of us." Tarrant tried to imagine what his own future would be like if Miss Orchard's recent successes in dysteleonics research brought in the extra funds she expected. She had announced plans to return every member of the distant Clan to Earth, one way or another, and if that happened this part of Shad Island was destined to become one of the busiest and most bustling places in the South Pacific.

"You're ready for something new," Somerville said. "I knew you'd never make the grade as a farmer, but with me it's a calling. Have to go, Hal—I want to make use of this sunshine."

Tarrant nodded, suddenly uncertain of his ability to speak, and took the older man's hand. Somerville winked at him, smiling, then turned and climbed down on to the deck of his boat. Tarrant detached the nylon ropes and threw them down after him, and the boat immediately began to drift clear.

"One thing I meant to ask you." Somerville put one foot on the gunwale and leaned on his knee, slipping easily into his portrayal of a genial buccaneer. "Are you going to marry that girl?"

Tarrant spread his hands and grinned. "It isn't required."

"Not by her, perhaps—but I think you'd rather have it that way."

"I'd have to teach her what marriage means, first." Tarrant waved goodbye to Somerville and watched the boat until it had passed out of sight beyond the western horn of the bay. He turned and hurried ashore, anxious to get back to Myrah. So far they had found only one thing in common—that their previous lives had been lonely and unfulfilled—but in his view that was quite good enough for a beginning.

# C.J. CHERRYH

"C.J. Cherryh just keeps getting better and better" –
Marion Zimmer Bradley

## Angel with the Sword

From the moment Altair Jones hauls Mondragon into
her barge she becomes entangled in a deadly power
game. Fine-boned and fair, the mysterious Mondragon
looks like a high-born from the fabulous upper levels;
certainly he will not survive long in the putrid
underworld of the canal folk.

Against all her instincts, Altair determines to conceal
him from the assassins and fanatics who threaten his life.
But unless she can learn the truth about Mondragon,
there is nothing her extraordinary cunning or her
ferocious love can do to protect him.

"A rare treat...Cherryh is in top form" –
Roger Zelazny

*Available in October 1987*
**The Dreamstone**

# ROBERT SILVERBERG

## The Masks of Time

The year is 1999. Into a world gripped by visions of an imminent apocalypse drops the hypnotically charismatic Vornan-19, claiming to be a traveller from the year 2999.

The world is indeed ready for a sign, an omen. But is Vornan-19 truly the new messiah? Or is he, rather, an instrument of wanton and devastating malice?

## To Live Again

Once the world's most powerful man, Paul Kaufmann is the prize in a ruthless game of violence, sex and treachery played by those determined to succeed him. For Paul Kaufmann is dead, his soul stored in the Scheffing Institute waiting to be awarded to whoever is judged strong enough to use it.

But who knows what such a fearsome mind contains – and who can imagine the results if an error of judgement is made?

# JACK VANCE

*"One of the finest writers the science fiction field has ever known"* — Poul Anderson

*The Durdane trilogy*

## Book I
## The Faceless Man

The men of Durdane have long since relinquished the right to control their destinies. A torc clamped round their necks ensures obedience to the unseen, impersonal and pitiless rule of the Anome. At last a man is born who refuses to submit. Without a torc he is at the mercy of all around him, yet still he dares to challenge the unchallengeable, to confront the Anome. But first he must find him — for though all men obey his commands, no man knows his identity.
He is the Faceless Man.

## Book II
## The Brave Free Men

Durdane lies in the grip of the devilish Roguskhoi. Raping and pillaging in their thrust to her heartland, they annihilate all who cross their path. With spirits sapped by years of tyranny, the men of Durdane stand impotent. One man alone can save them, the musician Gastel Etzwane. But even he is unaware that worming through the land is a corruption more deadly than anything the Roguskhoi can inflict.

*Available in December 1987*
## Book III
## The Asutra

# TITLES AVAILABLE FROM
# VGSF

The prices shown below were correct at the time
of going to press (April 1987)

| | | | | |
|---|---|---|---|---|
| ☐ | 03995 7 | WITCH WORLD | Andre Norton | £2.50 |
| ☐ | 03990 6 | THE MASKS OF TIME | Robert Silverberg | £2.95 |
| ☐ | 04008 4 | HEGIRA | Greg Bear | £2.95 |
| ☐ | 04032 7 | THE FACELESS MAN | Jack Vance | £2.50 |
| ☐ | 03987 6 | NIGHT WALK | Bob Shaw | £2.50 |
| ☐ | 04009 2 | ANGEL WITH THE SWORD | C.J. Cherryh | £2.95 |
| ☐ | 04022 X | MISSION OF GRAVITY | Hal Clement | £2.50 |
| ☐ | 03988 4 | THE OTHER SIDE OF THE SKY | Arthur C. Clarke | £2.95 |
| ☐ | 03996 5 | WEB OF THE WITCH WORLD | Andre Norton | £2.50 |
| ☐ | 04010 6 | EYE AMONG THE BLIND | Robert Holdstock | £2.50 |
| ☐ | 04007 6 | STAR GATE | Andre Norton | £2.50 |
| ☐ | 03989 2 | TO LIVE AGAIN | Robert Silverberg | £2.95 |
| ☐ | 03999 X | YEAR OF THE UNICORN | Andre Norton | £2.50 |
| ☐ | 04053 X | THE BRAVE FREE MEN | Jack Vance | £2.50 |
| ☐ | 04096 3 | MEDUSA'S CHILDREN | Bob Shaw | £2.50 |
| ☐ | 04011 4 | EARTHWIND | Robert Holdstock | £2.95 |

## Also available: GOLLANCZ CLASSIC SF

| | | | | |
|---|---|---|---|---|
| ☐ | 03819 5 | THE SIRENS OF TITAN | Kurt Vonnegut | £3.50 |
| ☐ | 03821 7 | MORE THAN HUMAN | Theodore Sturgeon | £2.95 |
| ☐ | 03820 9 | A TIME OF CHANGES | Robert Silverberg | £2.95 |
| ☐ | 03818 7 | NOVA | Samuel R. Delany | £2.95 |
| ☐ | 03849 7 | THE CITY AND THE STARS | Arthur C. Clarke | £2.95 |
| ☐ | 03850 0 | THE DOOR INTO SUMMER | Robert Heinlein | £2.95 |
| ☐ | 03852 7 | WOLFBANE | Frederik Pohl & C.M. Kornbluth | £2.95 |
| ☐ | 03851 9 | THE REPRODUCTIVE SYSTEM | John Sladek | £2.95 |
| ☐ | 03978 7 | A FALL OF MOONDUST | Arthur C. Clarke | £3.50 |
| ☐ | 03980 9 | A WREATH OF STARS | Bob Shaw | £2.95 |
| ☐ | 03979 5 | ROGUE MOON | Algis Budrys | £2.95 |
| ☐ | 03981 7 | MAN PLUS | Frederik Pohl | £3.50 |
| ☐ | 03993 0 | INVERTED WORLD | Christopher Priest | £3.50 |
| ☐ | 04061 0 | FLOWERS FOR ALGERNON | Daniel Keyes | £3.50 |

All these books are available at your shop or newsagent or can be
ordered direct from the publisher. Just tick the titles you want and fill
in the form overleaf.

VGSF, Cash Sales Department, PO Box 11, Falmouth, Cornwall.

Please send cheque or postal order, no currency.

Please allow cost of book(s) plus the following for postage and packing:

UK customers — Allow 60p for the first book, 25p for the second book plus 15p for each additional book ordered, to a maximum charge of £1.90.

BFPO — Allow 60p for the first book, 25p for the second book plus 15p per copy for the next seven books, thereafter 9p per book.

Overseas customers including Eire — Allow £1.25 for the first book, 75p for the second book plus 28p for each additional book ordered.

NAME (Block letters)................................................

ADDRESS................................................

................................................

................................................